FATA MORGANA

(Mirage)

Drawn by Lee Simonson

The Setting for The Theatre Guild Production of "Fata Morgana"

FATA MORGANA

(Mirage)

A Comedy in Three Acts
BY
ERNEST VAJDA

TRANSLATED BY
JAMES L. A. BURRELL
AND
PHILIP MOELLER

THE THEATRE GUILD VERSION,
WITH A DRAWING BY LEE SIMON-
SON AND TWO ILLUSTRATIONS
FROM PHOTOGRAPHS OF THE
THEATRE GUILD PRODUCTION

GARDEN CITY   NEW YORK
DOUBLEDAY, PAGE & COMPANY
1924

The cast of the THEATRE GUILD PRODUCTION as originally
presented at the GARRICK THEATRE, March 3, 1924

FATA MORGANA
(MIRAGE)
A Comedy in Three Acts
By ERNEST VAJDA
English version by James L. A. Burrell and Philip Moeller
The production directed by Philip Moeller
Settings and costumes by Lee Simonson
CHARACTERS (in order of appearance)

George	Morgan Farley
His Mother	Josephine Hull
Annie, his sister	Patricia Barclay
His Father	William Ingersoll
Peter	James Jolley
Rosalie	Helen Westley
Blazy	Charles Cheltenham
Mrs. Blazy	Armina Marshall
Therese	Aline Berry
Katharine	Edith Meiser
Henry	Sterling Holloway
Franciska	Helen Sheridan
Charles Blazy	Paul E. Martin
Mathilde Fay	Emily Stevens
Gabriel Fay	Orlando Daly

PLACE: St. Peter, on the great Hungarian plain known as the
Puszta.

TIME: Act I—An evening in July.
Act II—The following evening.
Act III—The next morning.

Fata Morgana is the Italian name of the fairy Morgan, step-
sister of King Arthur and pupil of Merlin. Her name is used to
designate the particular kind of mirage she is supposed to create,
which is frequent on the plains of Italy and Hungary. It is a
mirage of water, sometimes with ships and men.

Fata Morgana's other names are "Morgaine le Fee," "Morgue
la Fay," and "Morgan le Fay," which explains why Ernest Vajda
calls his heroine Mrs. Fay.

Stage Manager, James Jolley
Assistant Stage Manager, Paul E. Martin
The THEATRE GUILD, Inc.
Board of Managers

v

A PRODUCER'S PROBLEM

BY
PHILIP MOELLER

I sometimes think that writing about the art of the theatre is at a last analysis almost as futile as writing about music or indeed about any of the arts. The essence of the thing in most cases escapes the commentary, the map is never the country, and in a sense —and a very real sense at that—words are often the grave in which we bury our thoughts. How can any one ever really tell any one about music or pictures in spite of the fact that staggering reams of specialized data and historical fact be accumulated? Perhaps there is too much art. Unquestionably there is too much talk about it.

Now this is especially true in the theatre. There are too many dead essays about the living art of acting. We are bored and bothered too insistently with elaborate and travelled tomes about the art of the scenic designer. Our ears are so overcrowded with this over-emphasis of the importance of scenery that we are apt to forget the more important truth that the art of the theatre if it is anything at all is an art

that is alive at a given moment because of an interplay
of living elements that live at that moment and that
moment only.   Thus, in a technical talk even to spe-
cialists about a production one could exhibit charts
and give dimensions, but the coördinate result of words
and movement and light, the give-and-take of one
living instrument against the other, in fact the inner
rhythm of it all, this living thing which is the combina-
tion of all these living elements, dies in the attempt at
exposition, and at best we but hang an empty remnant
on the peg of a fulsome explanation.   And so this
brief word from the viewpoint of the producer will
have little or nothing to do actually with a discussion
of production but rather with the psychological problem which this play presents.

A play if it is a play follows its theme.   Even to-day
in the midmost of our extremist drama this is true.
The wildest ramifications of expressionism in the end
are apt to go somewhere, sometimes chaotically because
often in these plays chaos is the direction of the goal.
Any piece of work that merits attention has its innate
form, the theme is realized or not, but inevitably the
theme is there and if it be a fine one or a deep one and
if in its pregnant instances it touches universality so
much the more important is it.

The producer's first job is to understand the direction of the thought as the dramatist has set it spinning
and then to see that all that happens helps it spin.

Now the top usually turns one way but in some plays in mid-career it may somehow seem to stop and turn another. And this, though it may not seem apparent, is the rather secret and subtle problem in the production of "Fata Morgana." For here is a play about two people caught in a situation which results in a double dénouement. For Mathilde goes her spontaneous mondaine way to the tune of brittle laughter and George is poised for a moment on the brink of tragedy, poised for a moment only. For it would be unwise to take this terrible pain of the moment as true tragedy. True tragedy if it is worth its name has elements that must be a hurt forever, and George as he hears the train whistle over the Puszta and crowds back the agony that seems to be breaking his heart is a poignant rather than a tragic figure. Not that I would for a moment lessen the intensity of these terrible wounds of youth. We all of us have known them. We all of us have known how life has died on Sunday evening to be somehow miraculously and in our hidden hearts rather too alive on Monday morning. No, George is no Hamlet of the Hungarian plains; no Œdipus of adolescence. His problem the next morning from the viewpoint of a sympathetic and understanding inquirer who maybe remembers his own youth, if in any way it has been similar to George's, is a rather subtle one. How would George really feel? The answer to that is not perhaps the way we felt or didn't if somehow we can remember in our past some experience so fraught and so significant. For this problem though a universal one is at the same time always a special one, and our psychology in reaction to such a situation either of glamour or otherwise is always inevitably our own. As Vajda has conceived and written George, he is necessarily the George of the play, this particular youth of eighteen learning the first bitter lesson of disillusion. And if this first gleaming fairy that burnt with her beauty and her Eden-old spell into his naïve loneliness is now on her thoughtless journey back to Budapest and eventually to the latest things in bathing suits at Ostend, there is another and older and wiser and invisible fairy called Life still lurking about the room as the boy bends back to his school books. And if the cynic—and after all a cynic is one who hears the Truth so bitterly that he has to laugh lest he should cry—if the cynic listens he might hear Life telling the boy in a language which at the moment he cannot understand that the chances are more than even that when he goes up to the capital in the fall he is apt, oh yes ever so apt, to see again this lady of the mirage or some other lady who will symbolize the ever-present and ever-evanescent Fata Morgana of Love. And if again he recaptures the memory of the hot sands and the blinding blue sea of this night of the Puszta, the sentimental may sigh with a negating regret and the cynic still smile but this will not mean that his tragedy was either more or less because of this.

Thus Vajda to my mind has set the top spinning, this night of love, and a quick soon-over incident for the lady, this night of love and the seeming eternity of woe for the boy; thus the scherzo and the andante have for a space to play the melody together, two varying variations on the one tune, a difficult thing for a dramatist to write, a difficult thing indeed for the actors to play, and if I may say so not an easy thing for the producer to project. Yes, there is comedy here and, if one insists upon it, the shadow of tragedy, but not for George, for if one really is bent on finding tragedy the only person in the piece that even remotely touches the edge of its mood is Mathilde Fay herself, this exuberant, gay, and sudden lady who finds it so easy, ah so very easy! to laugh. This I take it is the gist of Vajda's theme; at least it was this producer's problem, though indeed one he may have created for himself.

INTRODUCTION

"Ihr naht euch wieder, schwankende Gestalten,
Die früh sich einst dem trüben Blick gezeigt."

Ernest Vajda (Vajda Ernö) was born in the year 1887 in Papa, the "Hungarian Heidelberg," whose college was the alma mater of Jokai, the novelist, and Petöfi, the lyric poet. The Vajda family moved to Komoron a few years later upon the death of the father, but young Ernest returned to Papa, where he was graduated from the college with the highest honours. Most of his vacations were spent with a classmate, the son of a farmer on the Puszta Ete. From Papa he went to Budapest to study law at the university at the wish of his mother, although his childhood ambition had been to become an actor and his first financial returns from a theatrical enterprise were from a marionette theatre which he evolved from potatoes, an ironing board, and other convenient requisites, charging the neighbours' children for admission to the performances.

Shortly after his arrival in Budapest, he had his first love affair—with a woman of about thirty-five, the prototype of Mathilde Fay in "Fata Morgana."

xiii

The law did not interest him and he attended lectures on literature and philosophy for four years, leaving the university without taking any examinations.

While he was still at the university, the waves of the Theatre Libre movement reached Budapest, where a group of actors and amateurs formed the Thalia Company along the lines of the Theatre Guild, which has given him his American triumph. Vajda was secretary of the Thalia Company and Alexander Hevesi, now director of the Hungarian National Theatre, its director. Hevesi had faith in Vajda from the first and encouraged him to write plays instead of poems, which had occupied him until that time. So he wrote his first play, "The Drive," and it was immediately accepted by the Thalia Company, which, however, went into bankruptcy before it could be produced.

Vajda then took the play to Beothy, director of the Magyar Szinhaz (Hungarian Theatre), who admired the play, but said that it was not according to his taste. Vajda asked him what sort of play he wished and, upon being informed, went home and wrote "Aunt Rosemary" within a week. Beothy fortunately had a toothache the evening the play was submitted. He sat up and read it, accepted and produced it within a month. Vajda was not quite twenty-one at the time. He contracted with Beothy for his next three plays and decided to expend more time and labour upon his next effort, as he had now decided to be a playwright.

He wrote "Ludas Matyi," an ambitious historical comedy, and dutifully took the script to Beothy, who accepted it as libretto for a musical comedy. The news was immediately published and the then director of the National Theatre summoned Vajda, read the play and accepted it. Vajda signed the contract gladly, having been chagrined that his serious literary work had been accepted as musical comedy material by Beothy. A dispute arose between the two directors and the play was finally produced in the National Theatre—an unprecedented success for an author of but twenty-two. The play was favourably received, but Beothy's powerful influence militated against it and the director of the National Theatre withdrew it, as he felt that his position was endangered.

Vajda next wrote "The Crown Prince," which treats of the affairs of the late Crown Prince Rudolph and Countess Vecsera, whose identities are thinly veiled. Beothy accepted the play, although its subject had aroused considerable comment; in fact Count Tisza, then prime minister, asked for a copy of the script, read it and forbade the production. Beothy refused to be deterred and young Vajda was summoned for military service with an intimation that he would not leave the army alive if a production took place; he withdrew the play and served but three weeks as a soldier instead of the obligatory year. Beothy renewed his option on "The Crown Prince" year after

year and it was finally produced in the Magyar
Szinhaz in 1923—twelve years after it was written.
It was also successfully given in Spain, but a projected
production in Vienna was forbidden by the present
Austrian Government.

Then came "Mr. Bobby," an extravaganza, which
was produced at the National Theatre, and "The Un-
expected Guest" at the Magyar Szinhaz. The latter
is a war play and was produced during the war, when
Vajda's pessimistic philosophy and evaluations were
not appreciated by the general public. A few years
previous, Vajda had won a prize for the best Hungarian libretto, "The Carnival Marriage," which was
not produced until a few weeks ago, as the composer
took nine years to write the music.

"Fata Morgana" was written in 1915. Although
the actual writing consumed but a short time, the play
had been maturing in the author's mind for years and
he had taken copious notes, as he had expressed his
intention of writing a play on the subject not long
after the termination of his first love affair. The
student Ernest Vajda is, of course, the prototype of
"George" in "Fata Morgana." The play was submitted to all the Budapest theatres, but none of them
accepted it, as Vajda's plays had not proven financial
successes. It was then sent to Copenhagen, where it
was most favourably received. Productions in the
various other neutral countries followed during the

war, though the news of these successes reached the author only after the Armistice.

Vajda was the editor of an illustrated weekly during the war years and also wrote short stories and contributions to the daily press, but always returned to playwriting. Since the Armistice he has written "The Confession," "Grounds for Divorce," and "The Harem," besides rewriting "The Crown Prince." Discouraged by the difficulty in having his plays produced in Budapest, he had "The Confession" given there under the name of "Sydney Garrick" as author. The belief prevailed that the play was an outstanding American success which Vajda had translated and it was received with acclaim not only in Budapest, but also in Vienna, Berlin, and in more than two hundred theatres in other places. The work was filmed and in a lawsuit over the film rights it was discovered that Vajda is the author.

Ernest Vajda is happily married and devoted to his wife and his son of seven years. His little family accompanies him even on short trips and his wife helps him in his literary work. He is bourgeois in his habits, except as regards finances. Like most Hungarians, he has great social gifts, and is a brilliant conversationalist when with congenial companions, otherwise diffident.

J. L. A. B.

NEW YORK CITY
March 12, 1924.

CAST OF CHARACTERS

GEORGE
HIS MOTHER
ANNIE, *his sister*
HIS FATHER
PETER
ROSALIE
BLAZY
MRS. BLAZY
THERESE
KATHARINE
HENRY
FRANCISKA
CHARLEY BLAZY
MATHILDE FAY
GABRIEL FAY, *her husband*

PLACE: Estate in St. Peter on the Puszta.

TIME: The first act takes place on the evening of July 26th, the second on the evening of the 27th, the third the morning of the 28th.

ILLUSTRATIONS

FATA MORGANA

ACT I

Photograph by Nickolas Muray

EMILY STEVENS AND MORGAN FARLEY IN ACT ONE
OF THE THEATRE GUILD PRODUCTION

FATA MORGANA

ACT I

[*SCENE: Large living room in an old-fashioned country house. In the background triple casement window arched above. Both sides are open wide. Potted plants on window-sill. Outside is a veranda; beyond, a flower garden. Flowers visible bordering veranda.*

The rear corner on the right of room is taken up by a vestibule, the door of which, when open, reveals a short flight of stairs leading down to entrance door of house.

On the right are two doors; the first, toward the proscenium, leads to the other rooms of the house, the second, to George's room. At the left, front, door to the guest room. A stove above it.

Old-fashioned furniture. At the left between the door to the vestibule and the guest room door—standing out a little from the wall, a large family sofa with slanting back. It is an old-fashioned piece of furniture, so large that about six persons can comfortably

1

*sit on it. In the centre of the room is a large round
table, with chairs around it. At the right, front, small
sofa; between doors, left, quaint carved cabinet.*

*On the sofas, tables, and chairs, old-fashioned cro-
cheted lace. On the rear wall, an embroidered cloth
strip to pull the servants' bell.*

*It is July 26th, St. Anne's day, about half-past six
in the evening.*

*GEORGE is seated at the round table, centre, with his
back to the window and facing the audience. Across
the table lies a double-barrelled hunting rifle, a whip,
and a small, round hunting hat. GEORGE is a slender,
black-haired, eighteen-year-old boy with girlishly re-
fined features. The blouse of his hunting costume is
unbuttoned. He supports himself with both elbows
on the table, presses his clenched fists to his temples,
bends over the book lying open on the table and learns
by heart; obstinately, with defiant bitterness. He
reads rapidly in a monotonous, loud voice.]*

GEORGE

"The man who first gave expression to philosophic
thought in the Hungarian language, he who first dared
to state that Magyarism, if it were to exist, must
strive for a real national culture, was John Csery of
Apaca, a poor, misunderstood, despised professor, who
died young." [*When he has finished this long sentence,*

which he babbled in one breath, he coughs loudly and begins at the beginning in the same manner, repeating it inaudibly] : "The man who first gave expression to philosophic thought in the Hungarian language——"

MOTHER

[*Simple, dignified, in a somewhat matronly "best dress" —but she has not entirely finished dressing—enters from the door up R. She closes the door behind her, stands still and looks at her son.*]

GEORGE

[*Looked up when the door was opened, now continues the interrupted sentence*] : ". . . garian language ; . . ."

MOTHER

[*Up R.*] :   George!

GEORGE

[*Stops studying, turns to her*] :   Yes, Mother!

MOTHER

What are you doing?

GEORGE

I'm studying.

MOTHER

[*Crossing to right of* GEORGE]: Go out in the garden and ask your father to forgive you.

GEORGE

[*Leaning over the book*]: "The man who first gave expression to philosophic thought . . ."

MOTHER

George! [GEORGE *stops.*] Didn't you understand?

GEORGE

[*Continuing, unmoved*]: " . . in the Hungarian language . . . was . . ."

MOTHER

If you don't ask your father, you can't come with us.

GEORGE

[*Shrugging his shoulders*]: Then I'll stay home.

MOTHER

[*Shocked*]: Your sister's first ball!

GEORGE

[*Obstinately*]: If it's all the same to Father . . .

MOTHER

He is quite right to be angry with you. You were away from home two days. No one knew where you were . . . left us worrying and anxious . . .

GEORGE

[*Looking up*]: Please, Mother, dear, I didn't want to hurt any one.

MOTHER

Well, then, go on out and apologize to your father.

GEORGE

No, I can't do that.

MOTHER

[*Angrily*]: No? Well, then, stay at home! [*She exits through the first door down R.*]

GEORGE

[*Alone, waits a moment then doggedly begins again*]: "The man who first gave expression to philosophic

thought in the Hungarian language, he who first dared
to state that Magyarism, if it were to exist, must strive
for a real national culture, was John Csery of Apaca,
a poor, misunderstood, despised professor, who died
young.   The man who . . ."

ANNIE

[*Outside the window, up L. C.*]:   Sh! Sh!   [*Whispering*]:   George!

GEORGE

[*Turns round, then goes on reading.*]

ANNIE

[*Disappears from window, enters room from door
up R., crosses behind to George's left.*]

GEORGE

[*Looking up*]:   What do you want?   Annie, I have
to study.   [*Resumes his studies.*]

ANNIE

[*Throwing right arm round his neck*]:   George, be
sensible.   Ask Father to forgive you, then you won't
have to study and can come with us.

GEORGE

[*Looking at her*]:   Did Mother send you here?

ANNIE

No.

[*Pause.* GEORGE *looks questioningly at her. She hesitates*]:

What are you thinking of? Mother told me that . . .

GEORGE

[*Pushing her off*]: You're as sly as a cat . . . you little liar. Go away!

ANNIE

[*Almost crying*]: I only wanted you to come to the Anna Ball. How do you like my dress?

GEORGE

You'll have a very good time there without me. [*Bitterly*]: It won't be the first time that you got along without me. . . [*Angrily*]: I didn't do anything wrong . . .

ANNIE

You didn't come home for two whole days. [*Sits chair left of table.*]

GEORGE

There was no reason for Father to shout at me: "You're not going to the Anna Ball with us! A

student who's failed belongs home with his books!"
So I'll stay home . . .

ANNIE

I'm going all right! Without you! And I'll have
a good time, too . . .

GEORGE

[*Burying himself in his book without further attention to her*]: "The man who first gave expression
to . . ."

ANNIE

[*Mocking him—repeats what he says.*]

FATHER

[*Elderly, deliberate, in black, with a long pipe, enters from up R.*]: Go on, Annie, help your mother
finish dressing. You'll all be late.
[ANNIE *exits hurriedly down R.* GEORGE *studies with
fearful zeal, muttering.* FATHER *walks across the
stage, behind* GEORGE *to left, casting side glances
at his son, expecting him to take the lead. As
nothing happens, he himself prepares to say the
first word, but he suppresses his friendly impulse*

at once, walks to the background and looks out the window. Pause.]

PETER

[*An old coachman with a long moustache, in his best clothes, enters from the hall up R.*]: Sir . . .

FATHER

[*Up L. To* PETER]: Have you harnessed the horses?

PETER

[*Up R.*]: That's why I came. Which carriage shall I use?

FATHER

Which carriage! We only have one.

PETER

[*Nodding slowly*]: I know that, sir.

FATHER

Then why do you ask?

PETER

I just thought . . . perhaps I ought to take the wagon.

FATHER

[*Going for him—annoyed*]:   Are you crazy?   The wagon?

PETER

Sir, it's only five minutes to the railroad . . . and then I could drive right on to Tahi-Nagyszollos. . . .   Because I have to drive over to-morrow morning for the barrels anyhow.

FATHER

That's to-morrow morning.   Before to-morrow morning you have nothing to do there.

PETER

Nothing to do—a—and at home neither.

FATHER

[*Anticipates what the coachman wants, peevishly*]: You have to watch the house.

PETER

[*Grinning*]:   Yes, of course.   But if the young gentleman's going to stay home . . .   then some-one'll be here anyhow to . . .   [*Pointing with his thumb to* GEORGE, *in a lower tone*]:   Or isn't he going to stay home?

FATHER

[*Looks at* GEORGE, *a momentary pause, then to*
PETER]: What do you want to do in Tahi-Nagyszollos? You won't get the kegs until to-morrow morning.

PETER

[*Outraged*]: But, sir, there's an Anna Ball there
too! It only comes once a year! [*He waits, short
pause*]: Sir, shall I take the wagon?

FATHER

[*Looking at* GEORGE]: I don't know yet. Ask
me later.

PETER

[*Looking at* GEORGE]: Sir, there is not much time
left.
[*He exits to the right grumbling.* FATHER *goes up L.
The moment* PETER *has disappeared, the noise of
approaching carriages, barking of dogs and the
sound of voices are heard.*]

MOTHER

[*Enters down R. dragging after her* ANNIE, *who
is red from the exertion of fastening her mother's
dress behind.* MOTHER *goes to the window up C.*]:
Heavens! . . . The Blazys! And we're not even

ready . . . [*Angrily to* ANNIE, *who is tugging at her dress*]: Hurry up or I'll have to call Katherine. . . . [*The carriage has stopped outside*]: Where is she? [*Calling*]: Katherine! Katherine!

ANNIE

She's been dressing Franciska for two hours. [ANNIE *lets go the dress, hurries to door down L., and calls*]: Franciska! Franciska!

ROSALIE

[*Enters from down L.*]: Is the house on fire? What are you screaming for, Annie? Franciska'll be ready in a minute.
[*She withdraws.*]
[BLAZY, MRS. BLAZY, *and* THERESE *enter from up R.*]

BLAZY

[*An elderly provincial in black*]: Hello! Are the young people impatient? It's hot! [*He chucks* ANNIE *under the chin, kisses her, then he looks questioningly at* FATHER *and sits chair up stage L.* FATHER *sits upper end of sofa, left.*]

MOTHER

How are you, my dear? Was it very warm driving over? [*Etc.*]

Mrs. Blazy

[*Dressed up, kisses* Mother, *and goes down R. to sofa*]: How fearfully hot it is! [Therese, *a young, overgrown girl, exchanges kisses with* Annie.]

Therese

This heat is simply . . .

Annie

It's so nice to see you . . .

Mother

[*Left of sofa R. to* Mrs. Blazy]: Sit down, please. [Mrs. Blazy *is about to protest.* Mother *does not let her speak, and pushes her down on the sofa*]: Just a moment—then we'll all drive to the station together.

Mrs. Blazy

[*Seated right of sofa*]: Well, just a moment, so as not to hurry you. Oh, this heat! [*Fanning herself.*]

Mother

A glass of wine—a little cake, my dear. [*Calling*]: Katherine!

Mrs. Blazy

[*Already protesting*]: No, I can't permit that. We won't eat anything now, nothing at all.

MOTHER

[*Crosses to cabinet R. for glasses*]:   Just a little cake, my dear . . . Katherine!

KATHERINE

[*The maid, grotesquely arrayed for servants' ball*]: Miss Franciska, ma'am, can't get her dress on, and she . . .

MOTHER

Never mind Miss Franciska.—Come here with me. [*She exits through veranda and off L. KATHERINE follows her.*]

ROSALIE

[*Rushing in from down L.*]:   Katherine, where are you going? [*She notices the guests, stops C., looking at* MRS. BLAZY.]

MRS. BLAZY

Well, so you are here . . . I thought so right away, when I heard them call Franciska. . . .

ROSALIE

Yes, we're here. We came last evening. [*Proudly*]: From Klausenburg. [*Sits right of table C.*]: Right from Klausenburg.

Mrs. Blazy

[*Enviously*]: In the city, in the middle of summer . . . I don't envy you.

Rosalie

Well, well! . . . But how we were entertained there! Three whole weeks.
[Mother *returns with cakes, followed by* Katherine *with wine.* Katherine *mumbles all through this.* Therese *and* Annie *ad lib. upstage.*]

Mother

Just a bite, my dears, before the ride. Katherine! Hurry! [*She points to left.*] Lock up everything and give me the keys. [Ad lib. *to* Mrs. Blazy.]
[Katherine *goes back to the left. When she comes to the window she exclaims with fright, for* Henry, *a young peasant boy, sticks his head up from, under the window-sill, where he had apparently been hiding, and threatens* Katherine *with his fists.*]

Katherine

[*Screams*]: Oh, horrors!
[*Everybody turns around and suddenly stops talking.* Henry *stands outside on veranda.*]

MOTHER

What was that?

KATHERINE

[*Moves over L.   Greatly embarrassed*]:
Nothing . . . madam . . . oh . . . nothing
. . . nobody . . .

BLAZY

[*Rises up C. at window*]: Henry! [HENRY *is
silent. Taking his ear*]: Didn't I tell you not to
budge from the house? If I find Charlie's run away,
I'll skin you alive to-morrow.

HENRY

Well, all right.   [*Exits L.*]

BLAZY

Such a good-for-nothing.   [*Returns to chair up L.
and sits.*]

MRS. BLAZY

[*Seated right of sofa R.   To* MOTHER]: How are
you going to get to Gabroc on the early train now?

ROSALIE

[*Seated right of table*]: We intended to, but it
pleased Mr. George—[*Looks at* GEORGE]—only half

an hour ago to put in an appearance from somewhere at the end of the world. [*All look at* GEORGE. GEORGE *gazes at his book.* ROSALIE *continues the chatter.*] And that was a piece of luck, too, for otherwise we wouldn't have got to the Anna Ball at all. As it is we must leave now by the last train and in ball dresses.

MOTHER

Yes, but . . .

ROSALIE

[*To* MOTHER]: Heaven forbid that I should criticize your method of bringing up children, but I tell you, if it were my son . . .

BLAZY

[*To* GEORGE]: And where were you those two days? [*Pause.* GEORGE *is silent.*]

FATHER

[*Seated left of* BLAZY *on sofa. Sternly to* GEORGE]: Don't you hear?

GEORGE

[*Without looking up*]: I was at the river.

ROSALIE

On the river—um-hm . . .

FATHER

[Learning for the first time where the boy has been, starts angrily]:   On the rafts?

GEORGE

I promised I wouldn't go to the rafts again.

ROSALIE

Indeed!

FATHER

[Calmed, also a little proud of the defiant answer, to BLAZY*]*:   If he's once promised, he won't go again. *[In a lower tone, explaining to* BLAZY*]*:   Last year the Slovaks knocked a young fellow dead.   When the planks are once unloaded, then they drink like fish. *[He calls attention to* GEORGE *with a movement of his head]*:   And he's always going to the river   .   .   . two hours away   .   .   .   *[To* GEORGE, *in a more forgiving tone]*:   Well, where were you on the river?

GEORGE

On the boat, with the fishermen.

FATHER

Did you eat there, too?

GEORGE

Yes.

FATHER

And sleep, too?

GEORGE

Yes.

FATHER

On the water?

GEORGE

On the water.

FATHER

Last year there was a bad fight between the Slovaks and the fishermen. [*He sighs.*]

BLAZY

This year, too. [*Jocularly*]: What's the use of troubling about a boy like that? We weren't any better ourselves. [*Looking at* GEORGE]: And then you've only got to look at him.
[ROSALIE *laughs.*]

FATHER

[*Quietly, proudly*]: He won a prize in weight-throwing at the county games this year.
[KATHERINE *enters down L. Crosses to right.*]

MOTHER

Oh, Katherine, did you lock up all the closets?
[KATHERINE *hands keys to* MOTHER.]

KATHERINE

Yes, ma'am.
[MOTHER *puts keys on the metal rings she carries.*
KATHERINE *locks the door down R., and gives the
key to* MOTHER.]

ROSALIE

Have you still the mania to lock every single door in
the house?

MRS. BLAZY

[*Shaking her own large bundle of keys*]: We simple
Hungarian women are used to it that way, Rosalie.

KATHERINE

[*At the door of* GEORGE's *room, up R.*]: Shall I
lock this door too, ma'am? [*She opens the door to
take the key from the inside.*]

ANNIE

[*Up R.*]: You don't need to lock that. George is
going in there to his feather bed.
[KATHERINE *crosses to L. Busy with lunch packages.*]

Therese

[*Up R.*]:   Isn't George coming with us?

Father

[*Looking at* George]:   It looks that way.

Therese

Charlie isn't, either!   He's sticking at home with his books too.

Mother

[*Down R.   Speaking with* Mrs. Blazy, *but looking at her husband*]:   And what did Charlie do?

Blazy

[*Seated, chair up L.*]:   A pupil that's failed has no business at the Anna Ball.

Father

And Charlie only failed in the seventh.   But George
———

Mother

[*Sighing*]:   Yes, George is preparing for his finals.

Peter

[*Enters from up R., and shouts from porch*]:   And I told you there was no time.

MRS. BLAZY

[*Rises, goes up R.*]:   Yes, let's go!

ROSALIE

It's not so late.   [*Looks toward the left at Franciska's door.*]

ANNIE and THERESE

[*Impatiently up to door R. and exit with* PETER]: Let's go!   Let's go!

FRANCISKA'S VOICE

[*From the left*]:   Katherine!   Katherine!

ROSALIE

[*Rises. To* KATHERINE]:   Go on in!   Help the poor little girl dress!

MRS. BLAZY

[*Coming down R.*]:   *So* we must wait for Franciska?

ROSALIE

[*Turning to* MRS. BLAZY]:   Franciska's putting on a new dress.   She got it from Budapest.

MRS. BLAZY

[*Behind sofa R.*]:   With her experience she ought to be ready anyhow.   She's been going to balls for

twenty years. The train will go without us on her
account.

ROSALIE

[*Breathlessly*]: Twenty . . . [*Contemptuously*]: Provincial!
[BLAZY, *who has been talking to* FATHER, *looks up.*]

MRS. BLAZY

[*Rudely*]: Well, what are you?

ROSALIE

[*Right of table. Taking her up quickly*]: I—provincial! We live the entire year in large cities. Klausenburg, Grosswardein, Debrecin! [*Playing her trump
card*]: And we spent last Christmas in Budapest.

MRS. BLAZY

[*Whom that really hurts, moves down R.*]: Of
course, when one does nothing else for thirty years except keep on visiting relatives. . . .

ROSALIE

Excuse me! We are welcome everywhere, they send
for us . . .

MRS. BLAZY

[*Mockingly*]: Ah, who sends for you?

MOTHER

[*Calmingly to* MRS. BLAZY]: Why, Malchen . . .

ROSALIE

[*Rising with her hands on her hips*]: They send for us; for we bring along culture, the latest style. We at least know how to talk like civilized and cultivated people.

MOTHER

Rosalie, stop, please . . .

MRS. BLAZY

They endure you! I tell you—you spend all your time visiting relatives. I said it once and I'll say it again.

MOTHER

That's enough now . . . Malchen!

ROSALIE

Hold me or something'll happen! [*Sits right of table.*]

MRS. BLAZY

Yes, they endure you!

BLAZY

[*Rises,* FATHER *pulls him down again*]: Wife, keep quiet now!

Rosalie

My poor, dear, departed husband, Koloman.

Mother

Yes, Koloman.

Rosalie

If he were living now . . . then no one would dare to insult me.

Mother

[*Calming her*]: Now don't cry, we believe you.

Rosalie

[*Her tears flowing copiously*]: Yes, I know. You think just the same! We were here last year for the vintage . . . and now we've come for the Anna Ball. . . .

Mother

[*Speaking quite loudly*]: We're always awfully glad when you come!

Rosalie

I didn't notice that yesterday. You didn't want us— [*Pointing to the first door on the left*]—even to occupy the guest room.

MOTHER

Because that was intended for the people from Budapest. But now you have it.

ROSALIE

Of course. Because the people from Budapest didn't come. [*She suddenly stops weeping, breathes deeply, then, still more embittered, turning to* MOTHER]: You invited them! You were looking forward to them. But they left you in the lurch.

MOTHER

[*Angrily*]: They may still come!

ROSALIE

[*Seated right of table. Triumphantly*]: They didn't even write.

FATHER

[*Seated sofa L.*]: What's true is true. . . . They really might have written.

MOTHER

[*Between* MRS. BLAZY *and* ROSALIE]: But Gabriel's so busy. [*Sadly*]: Before, he used to come here once in a while. But since he's married . . .

FATHER

[*L. C.*]: He might have brought her to see us at least once.

ROSALIE

Oh! How handsome she is!

MOTHER

[*Animatedly*]: Do you know her?

ROSALIE

[*Nodding*]: Yes!

MRS. BLAZY

You do?

MOTHER

And you never told us before! Tell us, Rosalie.

MRS. BLAZY

[*Sits left of sofa R.*]: Where did you see her?

MOTHER

What did she look like?

MRS. BLAZY

When did you see her?

MOTHER

What's she like? Go on, say something.

ROSALIE

[*Strikes an attitude with aplomb, as she now feels herself the centre of interest*]: Well, we saw her in Budapest. Last Christmas. At the theatre . . .

MRS. BLAZY

[*With curiosity*]: Where did you sit?

ROSALIE

[*Sweetly*]: In a box! Where fashionable people sit. [*Proudly*]: And we didn't pay anything, Cousin Anna. Our seats were given to us. Cousin Steffi . . .

FATHER

[*Impatiently*]: But Gabriel's wife—what's she like? [BLAZY, *up C.*]

ROSALIE

Well, there below us in another box sat a red-haired woman . . .

MOTHER

Red-haired?

ROSALIE

Or blonde. A very suspicious colour, anyhow. And people were running in and out of the box during the intermission, and the red-haired woman laughed so loudly and her dress was cut so low . . . [*She looks at* ANNIE *and* THERESE. *The women put their heads together*] . . . that you could see clear down her back.

MOTHER and MRS. BLAZY

[*Together*]: Oh, my God! No!
[FATHER *and* BLAZY *listen to this.*]

ROSALIE

Yes . . . she leaned against the railing and talked in the boldest way to the men in the next box. It was scandalous. Everybody turned their opera glasses on her. Even I was shocked and I said to Steffi: "What sort of a woman is that?" "What!" Steffi said, "you don't know her? That's Councillor Fay's beautiful wife." Well, I nearly fell out of my seat. Then Steffi told me stories about her. Stories, I tell you. [*Looks round to see if the men are listening. The men are busy talking*]: A count makes love to her . . .
[FATHER *and* BLAZY *listen again.*]

MOTHER

[*Seriously*]: Listen, Rosalie. If you slander Gabriel's wife, we'll quarrel.

ROSALIE

But I'm only saying what Steffi said. He said, "Half Budapest is crazy about her." Beautiful? I said . . . her hair is dyed! Her face is painted! Her teeth are . . .

MOTHER

Rosalie!

ROSALIE

Well, they are. All Budapest women are gotten up that way! . . . Well, and the next day we looked up her address in the telephone book . . . and so I called on her with dear little Franciska.

MOTHER

So you could really see what she looked like up close —you mean thing. And did you see her?

ROSALIE

No, she was never home! But we saw the maid, though.

[MRS. BLAZY *laughs*.]

But we spoke to Gabriel once! He's always so very busy, too. "Relations?" he said. "Very glad. You want to see my wife?" he said. "Very glad." Ran away and left us standing there. We waited and waited but she didn't come.

MOTHER

[*Disappointed*]: So you didn't really see her at all!

ROSALIE

No, but you can depend on my good eyesight, I . . .

[GEORGE *has been listening with absorbed attention, since the conversation has been about Budapest people.*]

BLAZY

[*Going for him*]: Study, Georgie, don't listen when they talk about pretty women.

[GEORGE *blushes deeply and lets his glance fall angrily.*]

FATHER

[*With annoyance to* BLAZY]: Don't do that, he doesn't understand such jokes yet.

ROSALIE

. . . and then we left Budapest.

PETER

[*Appearing at porch from right.* ANNIE *and* THERESE *enter with* PETER]: Sir, are we leaving today?

MRS. BLAZY

[*Rises*]: Heavens! What time is it?

BLAZY

Nearly a quarter after seven!

MRS. BLAZY

[*Excitedly*]: And the train leaves at half past!

FATHER

Now don't get excited.
[ROSALIE *rises.*]

FATHER

It only takes five minutes to walk to the station.
[*But this calming remark is in vain. They begin to run wildly, hither and thither. Over-hasty preparations.*]

KATHERINE

[*Entering from down L.*]: Ma'am.

MOTHER

[*Comes to right of table*]: Oh! Thank Heaven! Have you finished?

KATHERINE

Oh! we've finished all right. And now Miss Franciska says the dress doesn't look good on her—and she's taking it off and going to put on another.

ROSALIE

Heavens! Franciska! [*She rushes into room down L.*]

ANNIE

[*Following* ROSALIE, *exits L.* THERESE *exits with* PETER *R.*]: Franciska!

ROSALIE

[*Crossing to left*]: Right away! Right away!

MRS. BLAZY

[*Looking desperately toward the left*]: But now we'll really be too late!

MOTHER

[*Crosses to L. C. calling*]: Now listen, everybody. On three we're going. [THERESE *runs on from R. and drags* BLAZY *off.*] I mean what I say. One, two.

Come on, whoever doesn't come, stays here! Three!
[*The whole crowd rushes at the same time to the door
up R. and exits.*]

ANNIE

[*While she runs, laughing*]:   Franciska! Franciska!
[*All have disappeared off R. Only* GEORGE *and*
FATHER *remain.*]

ALL

[*Shouting from outside*]:   Franciska!

ROSALIE

[*Runs on from L.*]:   Just a moment! Just a moment! [*Exits L. again.*]

FATHER

[*After a momentary pause, drops down to* GEORGE'S
left. Says quietly]: Will you promise not to go to the
fishermen again? And to make up to-morrow what
you missed yesterday and to-day?
[GEORGE *is silent.*]

Then you may come with us . . . Take your
suit and change it at Aunt Marie's.

PETER

[*Enters,* (THERESE *hanging on to* PETER'S *arm*) *standing at door R.*]:

PETER

Sir, what carriage shall I take?

FATHER

Well, George?

GEORGE

[*Defiantly*]: I missed two days . . . make it up in one day . . . I can't promise that.

FATHER

[*In sudden anger to* PETER]: Take the wagon!

PETER

That's what I done already.
[*He disappears,* THERESE *dragging him off.* FATHER *exits to the right without looking at* GEORGE.]

PETER'S VOICE

[*From outside*]: Ho, ha-ho! [*Snapping of the whip is heard.*]

ROSALIE

[*Running from down L. screaming. Exits up R.*]: Franciska! Come on or they'll leave without you!
[FRANCISKA *rushes in with garments in her hand. Knocks over chair left of table, replaces it, and runs out up R.*]

MOTHER

[*Entering hastily up R.*]: Heavens! The door there's open! [*She turns the key in the door of the guest room, she runs back. Her bunch of keys clatter when she puts on the new key. She notices* GEORGE.]

MOTHER

George . . . Oh . . . you-u-u-u——

VOICES OUTSIDE

We're going! Come along!

MOTHER

[*Gasping*]: Look after everything . . . do you hear? . . . shut the window at night . . . you can never tell . . . Oh my, this key . . . there's fruit jelly in the pantry . . . [*Kissing him*]: You ought to have asked Father to excuse you . . .
[*She runs out. Outside, noise of voices, laughing, then snapping of the whip, the wheels creak, the dogs begin to bark, the rattling of the wagon is heard from a greater distance, then suddenly deep silence.*]
[GEORGE *rises, goes up to window, looks off R. Then looks off upstage—then back again to R. Drops down to table, sees the book—sits same chair—*

starts to study—reads speech through. Rises, paces L. to R., studying with book in hand, returns to table and starts to write speech. Gets down to cue—"John Csery of Apaca." Charlie enters up L. Calls through window.]

Charlie

Ooooh! [George *does not hear. Still louder,* Charlie *calls*]: Ooh!
[George *hears and looks up.*]

George

Who's there?

Charlie

A ghost! [*Appears at the window.*]

George

Charlie!
[Charlie *jumps in at the window.*] How did you get here?

Charlie

[*Coming down R. C.*]: On my wheel . . .

George

Did you run away?

CHARLIE

You don't think I'd wait till Henry comes back?
[*He laughs*]: Now he can hunt for me home. Have
you a cigarette? [*Coming down R.*]

GEORGE

No. . . . [*Front of table.*]

CHARLIE

That's right. You don't smoke. Sh! [*He listens.
From afar the sound of an approaching train is
heard*]: Listen. [*Runs up to window, looks off
L.* GEORGE *crosses to left of sofa R.*]

CHARLIE

There it comes! [*He imitates the sound of
the train*]: Pff . . . pf . . . pf . . .
Ho-chopp! Shshsh! [*The train hisses and stops*]:
Now it's stopped! [*He shouts*]:

Puszta—St. Peter! A tenth of a second! [*The
sound of another train is heard*]: That's the Gabroc
express on the other track. [*The express train is
heard clearly. He whistles. The whistling of the express train is heard.*] It's scooting by . . .
Now the accommodation train's leaving . . .
[*The rushing of the express train dies down, the de-
parting accommodation train puffs faster and faster*]:

Come on, hurry up, come on now . . . Tsh
. . . tsh . . . tshtshtshtsh . . . tshtshtshtsh . . . Hurrah! Now the coast is clear!
[*Takes a step down R. C.*]

GEORGE

What do you mean?

CHARLIE

The freight train to Gabroc goes in ten minutes.
While it's being loaded, we'll climb onto the last car,
and in an hour and a half we're in Gabroc. Have you
got any money?

GEORGE

No. [*Crossing to front of table.*]

CHARLIE

Not even a gulden? [*He waits.* GEORGE *shakes his
head*]: . . . A crown? . . . [*He waits.*]

GEORGE

[*Angrily*]: No, I tell you! Nothing!

CHARLIE

[*Coming down R. Bitterly*]: Oh! What the hell
did I wait for the train for?

George

Well, what are you going to do in Gabroc?

Charlie

[*Hoping again, ingratiatingly*]: George, I say, isn't it the limit? [*Crosses to right of table*]: They've all gone away and left me here alone because I wouldn't study. As if I could help it that the ass flunked me in Latin. He's jealous of me—[*Puts hands in pockets*] —because the cashier in the café likes me better. [*He winks*]: And it wasn't your fault either that another examination in . . .

George

[*Seriously*]: It was my fault.

Charlie

We're no longer children. We need freedom, freedom—[*With eyes lighting up*]—and women!

George

[*Grasps his arm, with glowing eyes*]: Charlie, let's go to Gabroc! To the Anna Ball! Now we *will* go! Do you want to?

Charlie

To the Anna Ball? And have my father drive me out of the house to-morrow?

George

[*Looking at him in astonishment*]: What do you want to do in Gabroc?

Charlie

[*Again in the previous ingratiating tone*]: In the Central Café there . . . there's a cabaret from Budapest . . . Girls, I tell you! The head waiter told me they'd sit at your table . . . You pay for their drinks, and then . . .

George

[*Hoarsely*]: And then?

Charlie

[*Puts hands on* George's *shoulders. Whispering*]: And then you can go home with them. [*He gives* George *a sidelong glance.*]

George

[*Breaking out*]: Gee! [*Pause.* Charlie *winks.* George, *roughly*]: Now keep your mouth shut!

Charlie

[*Taken aback*]: You mean you don't want to? . . .

George

I don't go to such dirty night joints.

Charlie

[*Bitterly*]:   Then come with me to **Mihalyfalva**!

George

What's going on there?

Charlie

The peasants' Anna Ball.   There are girls there, too, from all over.   [*Crosses to* George, *slowly*]: Fine young Slovak girls.   [*Whispering*]:   And Henry says they're crazy about students!   . . .

George

[*Shouting*]:   I'm not going anywhere.   **And now** get out or   . . .

Charlie

[*Crosses quickly to door up R.   Turns*]:   **Oho, you** think I don't know why you won't come?

George

[*Stands gasping at the near side of the table*]: **Get** out!

CHARLIE

[*Mockingly*]: You're no man at all. Your moustache isn't even beginning to grow. You 'fraid-cat! Now I see that you deserve your nickname!

GEORGE

I'll knock your head off!

CHARLIE

[*Mockingly*]: Miss Georgie! Miss Georgie!
[GEORGE *rushes after him.* CHARLIE *disappears from the door.* GEORGE *is about to run after him, controls himself.* CHARLIE *appears again at window, crying*]: Miss Georgie!
[GEORGE *grasps the gun from the table.* CHARLIE *runs away, head over heels, but from a distance shouts long-drawn-out*]: Miss Geor-gie!
[*Then the sound of a bicycle bell is heard. Then silence.*]

GEORGE

[*Alone. Up C. at window, comes down, throws gun on table*]: Rotten. I must get away from here.
[*Sits C., picks up book to study. Sits chair right of table. Starts to study, then throws book on table, book slips on floor. He rises, goes into his room R. Lights lamp in his room, comes back with a novel, and lights lamp over table, sits chair right of table and*

reads with pleasure. Puts down novel, picks up school book, starts to study aloud]: "He graduated from the University of Vilna in the year 1784, taking his doctor in philosophy five years later. He was called to the University of Copenhagen, where he taught Greek and Roman history for the next ten years." [*Loud barking of dogs outside*]:

He's coming back? Just wait! [*He grasps the whip, the barking becomes very loud. An anxious, thin cry of a woman is heard.* GEORGE *jumps up in alarm, listens a moment, then rushes to the hall door, jerks it open and shouts in a ringing voice*]: Keep quiet! Karo! Cæsar! Quiet! Quiet! [*He snaps the whip. The barking suddenly ceases. Deep silence.* GEORGE *calls*]: Who's there?

[*He is about to go out, but suddenly stands still as if petrified and lets the whip fall from his hand. In the doorway opposite to him appears a strange young woman in a handsome travelling gown.*]

MATHILDE

[*Gasping from running and from fear, enters and collapses stool left of door, up R.*]: The dogs . . . oh! the dogs . . .

GEORGE

[*Right of door. Stands there with his arms stretched out, even his fingers spread apart, after he has let the whip fall. He gazes at the woman without understanding, cannot speak a word. From outside renewed barking.*]

MATHILDE

Oh . . . They're coming . . .

GEORGE

Please . . . please . . . don't be afraid . . . they're not coming in . . .

MATHILDE

[*Looking at the open door*]: The door . . . Shut the door.
[GEORGE *pushes the door shut with his foot. Barking, then deep silence. The woman starts, then calms herself a little. She has not yet looked around, is still quite overcome from the fear she has experienced. Pause. She rises.*]

GEORGE

[*Sees that he must at last come away from the door. He takes a step toward the woman, then immediately steps back in dismay*]: Whom . . . please . . . whom are you looking for?

MATHILDE

[*Only now really notices* GEORGE's *presence*]: Who . . . who are you?

GEORGE

[*Bowing awkwardly*]: George. [*Quickly*]: George
Peredy . . .

MATHILDE

[*Laughs because she was so frightened and is suddenly quite calm and in a good humour*]: Excuse me
. . . I'm a little frightened. [*Looking toward
outside*]: But it's so curious . . . the whole
thing . . . You are surely my cousin . . .
aren't you?

GEORGE

I—I?

MATHILDE

Of course. [*Extending her hand*]: I am Mrs.
Fay. Gabriel's wife. I've come to see you.

GEORGE

[*Grasps nervously the gloved hand of the woman,
quickly lets it go again*]: To . . . to see us?

MATHILDE

[*Surprised*]: Of course to see you. Why didn't
you send a carriage to the station? Why didn't any
one meet me when I got here? Only the dogs! [*She
laughs*]: A friendly reception that, I must say.

[*Suddenly alarmed*]: Oh! Good Heavens! Perhaps you didn't receive my telegram?

GEORGE

Telegram? No. If my parents had received it, they wouldn't have gone to the Anna Ball.

MATHILDE

Are they already at the ball?

GEORGE

Yes . . . they've already left, just a few minutes ago.

MATHILDE

Oh, but that is extremely unpleasant. That telegram! I really don't understand . . .

GEORGE

Where did you telegraph to? We have no station here . . . The telegraph office is in Gabroc.

MATHILDE

I don't know. My husband telegraphed! [*Pause, looking at* GEORGE]: Well, what shall I do now? Perhaps you'll be so kind as to send for Cousin Anna——

[GEORGE *tries to interrupt.   The woman does not wait
for his reply*]: Oh no . . . [*Rises. Comes to
right of table*]: Why should we disturb her? The best
thing will be for me to meet them there. . . . We'll
surprise them! I'll change my clothes quickly. . . .
[*Taking off gloves and putting purse on table*]:
Heavens . . . My luggage is still at the station
. . . Won't you send for my things? Oh yes, the
check. [*Takes check out of her hand bag*]: Here it
is.

GEORGE

[*Comes to her right. Takes check, stands there
helplessly*]: Whom shall I send?

MATHILDE

Whom? The man. Or the maid. Or whomever
you wish. [*Sits right of table.*]

GEORGE

But there's no one at home. Besides me there's not
a soul in the entire house.

MATHILDE

They've all gone? [*Hesitating*]: Well, then
. . . [*Suddenly*]: Please, send for Cousin Anna
at once . . . or perhaps, if there's no one here

. . . won't you be so kind as to go yourself? . . .
But shut up the dogs first!

GEORGE

Please . . . please remember . . . [*With
sudden surprise*]: Did you come just now on the
train?

MATHILDE

[*Surprised*]: Why, how else? I came on the half-
past seven train from Budapest.

GEORGE

Yes . . . but then . . . I don't understand . . . Didn't you meet my family?

MATHILDE

Where?

GEORGE

At the station.

MATHILDE

Were they at the station? Did they expect me
there?

GEORGE

No. But they got on the train.

MATHILDE

On my train?

George

They left for Gabroc on the half-past seven train from Budapest. The same train that you came on. You must have got out on the right side instead of the left.

Mathilde

It's possible. I looked for someone . . . but there was only one man there, far away . . . up front . . . he was dragging a trunk . . .

George

That was the baggage man. He went front to the baggage car . . . We only have one man at our station.

Mathilde

There isn't any station there at all. It's only a little shed. I looked for somebody—a carriage—but there wasn't a living soul anywhere around—and the baggage man didn't come back. Then I saw this house in the distance. I knew it must be yours . . . my husband had told me . . . and then I ran here . . . I could hardly see the road in the dark.

George

It always gets dark so suddenly here.

MATHILDE

[*Pause*]: Well, then, what shall we do now? Someone must bring my things here . . . I can't go to
the ball like this. [*Taken aback*]: You say your
family went to the ball on the train . . .

GEORGE

Yes.

MATHILDE

Where is this ball?

GEORGE

The Anna Ball is at Gabroc. A thirty-five minutes'
trip on the train.

MATHILDE

Over half an hour? Then I must change my clothes
there. I can't go on the train in a ball dress. Is
there an up-to-date hotel in Ga . . . Ga . . .

GEORGE

In Gabroc? Of course. The Ox. The ball takes
place there, too.

MATHILDE

Fine! Then we'll go there and I'll change my clothes
in the hotel.

GEORGE

That will be difficult.

MATHILDE

To dress? Why? It will be possible to get a room there?

GEORGE

That part's all right. But it will be difficult to get there. There are no more trains to Gabroc to-night.

MATHILDE

What?

GEORGE

The next one leaves at seven in the morning. And then the Anna Ball will be over.

MATHILDE

But I came for the Anna Ball! [*Pause*]: What did you just say, how far is that—er—that——?

GEORGE

Gabroc? Thirty-five minutes by the train.

MATHILDE

[*Calmed*]: Well, then, we can go by the trolley. But can we take my luggage along?

GEORGE

[*Cannot believe his ears*]: What . . . what did you say, Mrs. Fay? . . .

MATHILDE

In the trolley. [*Irritated*]: That's still going, isn't it?

GEORGE

Please, this is Puszta-Saint-Peter, not Budapest.

MATHILDE

Good Lord! What's your name?

GEORGE

George.

MATHILDE

Well tell me, George. Excuse me, I am quite confused. The long trip, and the strange reception—well, tell me—because I should like to know—how am I going to get to that Anna Ball?

GEORGE

That I hardly know myself.

MATHILDE

[*Makes another attempt, but after the vanished illusion of the trolley line, she has no more faith in success*]:   Motor car?
[GEORGE *shakes his head.*]
   Cab?
[GEORGE *makes a gesture of negation.*]
   There must be some sort of carriage?

GEORGE

Oh!   Yes, we have a carriage   .   .   .

MATHILDE

Well, thank Heaven!

GEORGE

But no horses.   Peter took them along.

MATHILDE

But there must be some sort of vehicle?

GEORGE

[*Has a sudden idea*]:   One   .   .   .   yes   .   .   . there is one   .   .   .

MATHILDE

What is it?

GEORGE

I have a bicycle!

MATHILDE

Now George! Are you laughing at me?

GEORGE

I . . . excuse me . . . Good Heavens . . .

MATHILDE

[*Angrily*]: Well then, why are you talking about a bicycle? Even if I could ride one . . . [*She breaks out laughing*]: I can't ride to the ball on a bicycle. You foolish boy!
[*He turns away, and sits left of sofa R.*]

GEORGE

[*Blushes under her glance, stammering*]: Well . . . of course . . . it was stupid . . . I only wanted . . . my intentions were good . . . for there's nothing else . . .

MATHILDE

[*Becomes serious*]: Ridiculous situation! [*With renewed hope*]: Perhaps at a neighbour's . . . a carriage . . .

GEORGE

We have no neighbours. Only the Blazys, about ten minutes from here. But there's no one there either. They've gone to the Anna Ball, too. Their driver is with Peter.

MATHILDE

[*Quite desperate*]: But for Heaven's sake, there must be someone around the place.

GEORGE

[*Stuttering*]: Besides the station man . . . and Blazy's man Henry . . . we two . . . are the only people in several miles around.

MATHILDE

[*Rises. Looks at him*]: We two . . . in several miles . . .

[*Goes up and looks out of window, drops down to behind table. Almost raging*]: Oh, that idiot! I didn't want to come. But he'll pay for this spoiled day.

GEORGE

Oh, I . . .

MATHILDE

Oh, no, no. My husband! He insisted on this trip. It never would have occurred to me. But because he

has a case to plead to-morrow in that stupid Gabroc,
he insisted that I should come . . . He's coming
for me to-morrow . . . [*Raging again*]: Well,
just let him come! . . . But until then . . .
I'll be here alone . . . in the Puszta . . .
I'll never forgive him for that, never . . . [*Sits
right of table, her back to* GEORGE. *Pause*]: Will
there ever be anybody here again?

GEORGE

[*Very quietly*]: My family is coming home again
to-morrow morning.

MATHILDE

And all that time . . . all that time I must stay
here alone . . . the whole night . . . at the
end of the world . . . alone. Oh Lord . . .
[*She begins to sob bitterly, head in hands on table.*]

GEORGE

[*Desperately. Rises, goes to her right*]: No . . .
no! Please . . . don't cry . . . Mrs. Fay!
[*He dares for the first time to address her, in his zeal
he leans over her chair without noticing it*]: No
. . . I can't stand that . . . I'd rather
. . . yes . . . you see, I'll get on my
wheel . . .

MATHILDE

[*Laughing and crying*]: And you'll take me on your back, won't you?

GEORGE

[*R. C.*]: No . . . no . . . [*Beaming*]: Well, you're laughing again . . . But I'll go to Gabroc on my wheel, bring a carriage . . . and then you can go to the Anna Ball . . .

MATHILDE

[*Turns. Looks into his face*]: And how long would that take?

GEORGE

An hour and a half there . . . an hour and a half back . . . another hour and a half there. . . .

MATHILDE

That is to say, I'd arrive to-morrow morning . . .

GEORGE

Perhaps sooner . . . I'll hurry as fast as I can . . . [*Goes up R. to door, opens it. Dogs bark.*]

MATHILDE

And you'll leave me quite alone . . . in this fearful place . . . No! No! Don't go . . .

Don't leave me alone! Oh, I'm so miserable . . .
[*And her tears flow still more copiously.*]

GEORGE

[*Comes down to right of* MATHILDE *leans over her*]:
Please don't cry . . . I beg of you . . .
don't cry!

MATHILDE

[*Pauses.   Looks up, smiles under her tears, coquet-
tishly*]:   Does it hurt you to see me cry?

GEORGE

I can't look at you.

MATHILDE

Because you are a dear, sweet boy and not a disgusting egotist like . . .   [*She stops, then poutingly*]:
You won't think horrid things of me, will you?

GEORGE

I?   [*Shakes his head.*]

MATHILDE

You must think me a perfect monster . . .   I
burst in here, bad-tempered and dusty, and then I rave
. . . and rage . . .   and it isn't your fault at

all.   You are a dear, good boy . . .   I can see it
in your eyes . . .   You don't think badly of me,
do you?

GEORGE

[*Warmly*]:   No, certainly not. . . .   I couldn't
think anything bad of you.

MATHILDE

[*Looking up at him over her shoulder*]:   Really
not?

GEORGE

[*With the greatest candour, turns away, sits right of
sofa*]:   I didn't know you at all and still I didn't believe what they said about you.

MATHILDE

[*Surprised*]:   What?   You have already heard of
me?   Where?   From whom?

GEORGE

Here at home.   All sorts of bad things.

MATHILDE

[*Outraged*]:   Hm, nice relations.

GEORGE

No, no!   Don't think that!   Father and Mother
always praise you. . . .

MATHILDE

They don't know me at all.

GEORGE

But still they say fine things about you and are fond
of you and proud of you. But we have a relative here
now, an old lady with an evil tongue. She saw you in
Budapest . . . in a box at the theatre . . .
and she said . . . Oh I don't care what she
said . . . [*He stops.*]

MATHILDE

[*With curiosity rises, goes and sits left of* GEORGE]:
What? Well what? You can tell me. I won't be
angry.

GEORGE

[*Breaks out in childish laugh*]: That a count
makes love to you . . . that your hair is dyed
. . . even your teeth are false . . .
[*Both laugh.*]

MATHILDE

And you didn't believe that, did you?

GEORGE

[*Shaking his head*]: I couldn't believe anything
bad about you.

MATHILDE

And you tell me that right to my face?

GEORGE

[*Very warmly*]: I'll tell you everything . . whatever you want.

MATHILDE

[*Looking at him with delight*]: How old are you?

GEORGE

Eighteen!

MATHILDE

Eighteen! And tell me . . . George . . . what are you?

GEORGE

I'm your cousin, Mrs. Fay.

MATHILDE

[*Laughing*]: Quite right, George, I know that. But I mean what are you. What do you do?

GEORGE

I study.

MATHILDE

A student! But isn't that charming! And where do you go to school, here on the Puszta?

GEORGE

But I don't go to school. Not on the Puszta, but in Gabroc, to college.

MATHILDE

In what class?

GEORGE

I'm preparing for the final examinations now.

MATHILDE

Really? Why then, you'll come to Budapest next year.

GEORGE

[*Proudly*]: Of course. But first I must pass the examinations.

MATHILDE

When will that be?

GEORGE

In September. Only conditions. [*Defiantly*]: I flunked in June.

MATHILDE

[*Laughing*]: You flunked? Dear me, how delightful . . . [*Pause*]: George, if you knew what a good humour I'm in . . . [*With a roguish laugh*]: I'm not a bit sorry about the Anna Ball!

George

[*Beaming*]: No?

Mathilde

I feel so light . . . so gay . . . [*She stretches*]: It's nice here . . . this peace. . . . This great, beautiful peace . . . and you . . . are so kind . . . so young and so different from the others. . . . You know, I feel almost like a student myself. [*She laughs.*]

George

[*Happily*]: And you're not angry?

Mathilde

I? Angry? No. I am happy . . . I'm so joyful . . . [*She takes a deep breath*]: It's so nice here in the country. The air's so good. [*Looking at* George]: I don't know why it is. I am usually so reserved with strangers . . . and I know you scarcely half an hour and talk with you as if we were good old friends.

George

And I could never talk that way with anybody before, either!

MATHILDE

[*Extending her hand*]: Comrades! That's what we are, eh? Just comrades?

GEORGE

[*Taking her hand*]: Yes.

MATHILDE

I never felt so free before. [*Rises, goes up to window*]: What a glorious night! [GEORGE *rises, follows her, stands right of her*]: And how many stars! There's not nearly so many stars in Budapest. . . . [*Turns to him in a mysterious tone*]: And not a soul anywhere around!

GEORGE

No.

MATHILDE

Oh, I'm no longer afraid! It's wonderful to be so alone! And this quiet . . . [*With delight*]: Quite alone . . . no one sees me. . . . No one watches me. . . . No one torments me. . . . George, tell me. You can walk for an hour and a half and not meet a soul?

GEORGE

Not a soul. [*The dogs bark outside.*]

Mathilde

There's someone! See! Isn't there? There goes someone! [*She runs away from the window to the first door R.*]

George

[*Angered*]: Who can that be? At this time?

Mathilde

[*Tries to go out by the first door R.*]: Oh, it's locked! [*She looks for the key and doesn't find it. She rushes to the second door R., jerks it open, hurries in, and bangs the door behind her.*]

George

[*Looks after her in astonishment, not understanding why she has run away*]: But please . . . [*Renewed barking.* George *goes to the window and speaks outside*]: Keep quiet, Karo—Cæsar—Who's walking around here?

Henry

[*Appearing at the window*]: Only me, young gentleman. I wish you a good evening.

George

[*Roughly*]: What do you want here?

HENRY

The young gentleman . . . Charlie . . . ain't he here?

GEORGE

No. Good-night.

HENRY

All right. All right. I'm going, I don't have to be sent away.

GEORGE

[*Suddenly*] : Wait a minute. Where are you going?

HENRY

To the station. Maybe the young gentleman's there . . . looking at the trains.

GEORGE

[*Taking the baggage check from pocket*] : Henry, you'll get some luggage at the station for this check. Bring it here.

HENRY

Now?

GEORGE

[*Shouting*] : Now, of course. Don't you understand? Get along.

HENRY

All right!   I'll bring it.   You don't have to yell so.
[*Exit off L.*]

MATHILDE

[*Sticking her head out of the door*]:   Has he gone?

GEORGE

Yes.   [*Coming down to her left.   The woman comes
into the room.   *GEORGE* suddenly*]:   Tell me, why did
you run in there?

MATHILDE

[*Laughing*]:   Tell me, and why did you get rid of
him in such a hurry?

GEORGE

[*Blushingly*]:   I don't know.   Only I wanted him
to go to the devil.

MATHILDE

[*Pause*]:   Is that your room, George?   [*Looking
toward his room.*]

GEORGE

Yes.

MATHILDE

You have a lot of books.   [*Pointing to the first door
on right*]:   And where does that door lead to?

GEORGE

To my parents' room.   But Mother has the key.

MATHILDE

[*Crosses to door down L.*]:   And this one?

GEORGE

To the guest room.   [*Crosses behind table to right of her.*]

MATHILDE

[*Trying to open the door*]:   But it's locked too.

GEORGE

Mother always locks all the doors.

MATHILDE

[*Laughing*]:   What a charming custom!   [*Turning suddenly to* GEORGE]:   But where will I sleep, then?

GEORGE

Where . . . you . . . ?

MATHILDE

Where will I sleep?   I must sleep somewhere!

GEORGE

I . . . I don't know . . .

MATHILDE

And then I'd like to fix up a little, George. I'm just the way I was when I came from the train, quite dirty.

GEORGE

I . . . don't be angry . . . I am so awkward. . . . Your luggage will be here in a few minutes.

MATHILDE

Yes? That'll be very nice. [*Looking at table*]: But . . . may I be frank? . . . I'm awfully hungry. I haven't eaten anything since noon.

GEORGE

Oh . . . how stupid I am! [*He looks at her, laughing*]: I've never been host before! Please take some cakes. I'll get something else right away. . . . [*He runs to the porch.*]

MATHILDE

George! Where are you going?

GEORGE

[*With his hands on the window-sill*]: To the pantry. [*Exit through veranda to left.*]

MATHILDE

[*Laughing. Sits behind table*]: What a charming boy . . . this student!

[*Pause. Pieces of glass are heard falling.*] Heavens, what's that? [*Pause.*]

GEORGE

[*Enters with a dish of fruit jelly, plates, spoons, etc., in both hands, and puts them quickly on the table then stands left of table*]: Please, please, eat!

MATHILDE

Where were you? What made that noise?

GEORGE

The pantry door was locked so I pushed the pane in.

MATHILDE

Good Heavens! Has anything happened to you? Show me your hand.

GEORGE

No! [*Showing his hand. She takes it, caresses it slowly, sensuously. Long pause, then looks up at him, smiles*]: Please eat now.

MATHILDE

Gladly. But of course you must join me.

GEORGE

[*Sits left of table*]: Will you have some fruit jelly?

MATHILDE

[*Laughing*]: Fruit jelly? Why this is a centre of civilization!

GEORGE

[*Filling her glass*]: A little wine . . . from our own vineyard.

MATHILDE

Wine? [*She shakes her head*]: I don't drink wine. It goes to my head so easily. I'd rather have water.

GEORGE

You mustn't drink water with fruit jelly. It's not healthy.

MATHILDE

All right then . . . [*Laughing*]: But only a drop! . . . but of course you must join me.

GEORGE

Of course. [*Pours out wine, hands glass to* MA-THILDE.]

MATHILDE

[*Waits for him to toast, he doesn't, stands embarrassed. She smiles*]: Your health, George!

GEORGE

[*Rises, steps away from table, stands erect. Raises his glass*]:   Your health, Mrs. Fay.

MATHILDE

Don't say Mrs. Fay to me.   [*Pouting*]:   I'm not so old as that.

GEORGE

I bet you're younger than I am!

MATHILDE

[*Laughing*]:   You stupid boy!   I'm ten years older than you.   But that's no reason for you to say Mrs. Fay to me.   [*Both drink.*]

GEORGE

[*Puts down glass. Sits. Slowly and nervously*]: Well   .   .   .   what shall I call you?

MATHILDE

Mathilde, my first name.   [*Pause first, then clinking glasses with him*]:   Your health, George!

GEORGE

[*Intoxicatedly*]:   Yours, Mathilde!   [*They both drink.*]

long, because they treat me like a child. Nothing but
calling down . . . nothing but punishment . . .
and you . . . you were the first person in the world
who didn't treat me like a child . . . and now
you're beginning, too . . . [*Beseechingly*]: So
tell me . . . tell me frankly. . . . Am I. . . .
Am I a child?

MATHILDE

[*Looks at him a little taken aback and a little
amused*]: No . . . no . . . George . . .
[*Quickly*]: You are no child. [*Their glances meet,
she is silent, then she draws back a little from him,
slowly with a deep glance*]: I made a mistake. . . .
You are a man. . . . [*Pause. Dogs bark outside.
The woman jumps up*]: Someone else!

GEORGE

[*Rises, goes up to window*]: Henry's coming back
. . . with the luggage.

MATHILDE

[*Hesitates a moment, then runs into George's room.*]

HENRY

[*Pushing open the hall door*]: Here I am, sir!

GEORGE

[*Opening the door wide*]: Is it heavy?

HENRY

[*With a trunk on his shoulder and suitcase in one hand*]: No, it's light! [*He puts it down*]: The station man asked if that was personal luggage. He didn't see no one come.

GEORGE

That's no affair of yours. Look in to-morrow and you'll get something.

HENRY

All right, all right. . . . Well, good-night. [*Exits.*]

GEORGE

[*Calling*]: All right.

MATHILDE

[*Opens room door*, GEORGE *hands suitcase to her*]: Well, at last it's here.

HENRY'S VOICE

Mr. George!

MATHILDE

Oh my! [*Takes suitcase, exits quickly again.*]

HENRY

[*Is seen standing at window.*]

GEORGE

[*To* HENRY]: What do you want now, I told you to-morrow.

HENRY

Mr. George! Mr. Charlie wasn't at the station looking at the trains. There wasn't anybody at the station but the station man and he wasn't looking at the trains. Everybody's gone to the Anna Ball. Everybody but me and you and the station man. But Mr. George, Katherine . . .

GEORGE

[*Impatiently*]: What about her?

HENRY

Isn't she home?

GEORGE

No.

HENRY

Well, that's always the way. When you know the hens are under the hay, you can be sure they're somewhere else. Well—good-night.

[*Goes.*]

GEORGE

[*Turning around, sees that he is no longer there, crosses to door and with hesitation*]: Mathilde, he's no longer here . . .

HENRY

[*Appears again at this moment at the window*]: Mr. George! Mr. George, oh Mr. George, I was just thinking—well—maybe thinking isn't the word—maybe I should say *thinking*; but—Katherine—Mr. George—you say she isn't here?

GEORGE

No.

HENRY

Well, maybe she is away. But maybe away isn't just the word—well—good-night. [*Exits.*]

GEORGE

[*Going to the door*]: Mathilde, come. . . . [*He tries to open the door*]: You've locked it? . . . [*Pause*]: Please . . . Henry's not coming back any more. . . .

HENRY

[*Enters again and stands up R.*]: Mr. George! Mr. George! I want to ask you something. That is, *if* you don't mind. Mr. George—Mr. George—Did Katherine go to the Anna Ball?

GEORGE

Yes.

HENRY

I might have expected it. Maybe expected isn't just the word—but you go right on expecting just the same. She didn't tell me she was going. Mr. George —I want to ask you something. Is Peter here?

GEORGE

No!

HENRY

I wonder if that's why she didn't tell me she was going. I wonder about lots of things, Mr. George— lots of things—Well, what's the use of wondering! I'll ask her when she gets back. Mr. George—I want to tell you something—you won't mind, will you, Mr. George?

GEORGE

Well?

HENRY

I was at the last Anna Ball. Yes, and she was there, too—I mean Katherine—dancing all the time—all the time but not with me! Oh well, what's the difference?

One Anna Ball's just like another Anna Ball—all the
Anna Balls—all of 'em. So Katherine's gone to the
Anna Ball. Ah well—good-night!

[*This time he leaves for good. The key creaks in the
lock, the woman appears in a charming, coquettish
négligé, her hair is partly down.*]

GEORGE

[*Walks slowly toward her, then in an ecstatic tone*]:
Mathilde, how perfectly beautiful you are!

MATHILDE

Really? Do I look well?

MATHILDE

[*She walks past him, looking back at him coquet-
tishly over her shoulder*]: And my hair? [*Teasing*]:
Is it dyed?

GEORGE

Your hair? . . . Your hair. . . . I never in
my life saw anything like it. . . . I never dreamed
there could be such a miracle as you. . . .

MATHILDE

George, you're talking foolishly. . . . And I
oughtn't to listen to you at all . . . but this night

. . . [*Going up to right of window*]: and this air . . . it is so hot . . . and smells so strongly of flowers . . . I have no idea what it is . . . and it is quite benumbing . . . I don't recognize myself at all. Tell me, George, what is it . . . this warmth, as if I were on fire? For it's night . . .

GEORGE

[*Goes up to right of her. Quietly*]: It is the Puszta . . . It's been a very hot day. To-morrow there will be a mirage. . . .

MATHILDE

The Puszta! That sounds like something quite wild . . . something quite adventurous. . . . The Puszta! . . . Perhaps it is that. . . And this great, great fantastic solitude. [*Intoxicated, she turns quickly*]: Give me a little more wine, George. [GEORGE, *behind table, pours out wine. She laughs*]: It makes no difference if I do get a little dizzy. . . . [*Coming down to chair left of table*]: No one can see me here . . . can they . . . no one? [*She looks at him sharply.*]

GEORGE

[*Quietly*]: No . . . no one . . . [*Gives her wine. She drinks, hands back glass.*]

Mathilde

[*Sits left of table*]:   Aren't you sorry?

George

For what?

Mathilde

Because you must stay home?   Because they didn't take you along to the ball?

George

[*Behind table, stands facing her*]:   No, even if you hadn't come. . . .   But this way . . .   [*He stops.*]

Mathilde

But this way . . . tell me. . . . But this way. . . .?

George

You'll be angry.

Mathilde

I won't be angry.   Tell me. . . .   But this way?

George

No one in the world is as happy as I am. . . .

Mathilde

No one!   [*Looking down*]:   And I?

GEORGE

You. . . . Aren't you happy?

MATHILDE

[*Bitterly*]: I . . . with my empty life . . . at the side of a man who. . . . [*Pause*]: Didn't anyone expect you at the Anna Ball?

GEORGE

[*Does not understand*]: Who should expect me?

MATHILDE

A beautiful girl . . . or perhaps a beautiful woman, whom you wanted to dance with. . . .

GEORGE

No! No one . . . expected me. . . .

MATHILDE

Ah, now I understand. Of course. That's why you didn't go.

GEORGE

Why?

MATHILDE

Because she isn't there.

GEORGE

Who?

MATHILDE

She.

GEORGE

I don't understand.

MATHILDE

Look here, George, we're comrades . . . now come here . . . [GEORGE *moves to left of table, faces her*]: Be frank . . . There is a "she," isn't there? Whom you meet secretly . . . exchange kisses?

GEORGE

[*With consuming longing*]: I have never kissed a woman in my life.

MATHILDE

So . . . you've never been in love?

GEORGE

[*Wavering*]: Till now . . . never.

MATHILDE

And now?

GEORGE

Now . . .

MATHILDE

[*Whispering*]: Don't be afraid, George, don't be afraid of me . . .

GEORGE

[*Sinking down in front of her*]:   I love you!

MATHILDE

You love me? . . .   You love me? . . .   So
suddenly. . . .   You saw me to-day for the first
time, and you love me?

GEORGE

I love you.   I should like to die for you.

MATHILDE

Die? . . .   Ah . . .   they all say that. . . .

GEORGE

You don't believe me? . . .   [*He jumps to the
table, grasps the gun by the barrel and, bending it on
the floor, aims the double barrel at his temple and
touches the trigger.   He is half on his knees and looks
at the woman as if she were an altar picture*]:   **One
word** . . .   just say one word . . . and **I'll** pull
the trigger. . . .

MATHILDE

Oh, my God!——— George, for Heaven's sake . . .
[*Rises quickly.*]

GEORGE

If you wish it, I'll die . . . this minute . . .

MATHILDE

[*Trembling*]: George, put the gun away at once!

GEORGE

At a word from you . . . for you . . . and
I will be happy!

MATHILDE

[*She sits again, opens her arms to him*]: I love you.
[GEORGE *puts the gun on table. Sinks down and
embraces her, kneeling*]: This dear, beautiful head.
. . . [*She kisses him.*]

GEORGE

[*Embracing the woman, in ecstasy*]: Is this true?
Am I dreaming . . .?

MATHILDE

Yes, we're dreaming . . . both of us . . .

GEORGE

No . . . this is reality . . . and here . . .
and here. . . . [*He covers her with kisses.*]

MATHILDE

[*Closing her eyes*]: My George!

George

And still everything is a dream . . . a fairy tale.
They leave me here alone—for punishment, and then
—you come. And are here alone with me—that's why
I had to stay home. Fate. It meant that we should
be together. It was that, only that. I was so rest-
less yesterday. I couldn't sleep—early in the morning I ran away and hid myself in the reeds. I dreamt
of you—I saw your face like a light leading me. You
took me in your arms, just as now, and held me fast;
it didn't let me go away from home because I was to
meet *you, you, you.*

Mathilde

[*Benumbed by his warm words*]: No, no, never
mind, don't talk, don't talk! You dear, dear boy.
. . . If you knew . . . what you are giving me.
Life . . . No! more than life . . . Till now it
was nothing but disappointment. The tameness and
disgust! . . . nothing else . . . and I had to
come here . . . to find you. Your young . . .
pure soul. . . . [*She embraces him*]: Oh . . .
my husband . . . How I hate him!

George

Never . . . you'll never go back to him again.
. . . I won't let you! . . . To-morrow. To-
morrow I'll speak with Father. . . .

MATHILDE

[*Looking at him in surprise and pushing him gently away from her*]: What did you say?

GEORGE

I'll speak with Father . . . I won't study any more. I'll work on the farm . . . from to-morrow on I'll earn my living. . . .

MATHILDE

[*With curiosity*]: And then?

GEORGE

You'll stay here . . . forever . . . with me . . . on the Puszta. You'll divorce your husband and I'll marry you . . .

MATHILDE

What? . . . You! . . . You dear! . . . You . . . you . . . want to marry me! [*Laughing and crying*]: You sweet little fool!

GEORGE

. . . You'll divorce your husband!

MATHILDE

Yes, my dear, I'll divorce him. [*She laughs*]: If he insists.

GEORGE

[*Raging*]:   If he doesn't want to, I'll kill him!   I'll kill every man that only looks at you.

MATHILDE

My brave friend!

GEORGE

[*Holds her tightly*]:   We'll never part!

MATHILDE

Never.   Never.   [*Another embrace and then slowly pushes the boy away with a calculated movement*]: And now we must say good-night to each other   .   .   . it's so late   .   .   .

GEORGE

[*In a low tone*]:   Now   .   .   .

MATHILDE

I   am   tired   from   the   trip   .   .   .   so   .   .   . good-night, my dear friend   .   .   .   till to-morrow morning.   [*Pause*]:   Good-night.

GEORGE

[*Intoxicated, but like one who finds it quite natural*]: Good-night.   .   .   .   [*Crosses   to   door   up R.*]

MATHILDE

[*Rises, goes up to the window*]: First we'll close the window . . . [GEORGE *comes back to back of her, they close window*]: Everything is to stay outside now . . . the Puszta . . . the heat . . . the intoxication. . . . [*His hand touches hers, she draws hers away*]: No, no. In here we want to be nice and quiet now . . . and sleep. . . . I here . . . [*Pointing to the sofa*]: and you there. [*Pointing to the right.* GEORGE *goes R. to his room.* MATHILDE *comes down, sits behind table*]: And we'll leave the key on the outside! . . . [GEORGE *stops and turns to her.*]

GEORGE

[*Does not understand*]: Yes, Mathilde . . . [*He takes the key from inside the door and puts it in the outside.*]

MATHILDE

And study a little more. It's very important.

GEORGE

Good-night! [*Exits.*]

MATHILDE

Good-night!

GEORGE

[*Appears at the door with a large white pillow*]: Excuse me . . .

MATHILDE

[*Screaming*]: Oh, who is that . . . How dare you come in here?

GEORGE

Don't be angry. [*Comes to right of* MATHILDE]: But it occurred to me . . . here . . . like that. . . . [*Goes over to sofa, L.*] How will you sleep here? If you'll allow me, I'll make the bed.

MATHILDE

[*Laughing*]: Can you make a bed?

GEORGE

No, but . . .

MATHILDE

Well, what are you doing?

GEORGE

At least . . . this pillow . . . [*He lays the pillow on the sofa and strokes it tenderly with his hand.*]

MATHILDE

You . . . you mustn't stay any longer now.
Go . . . go to your room.

GEORGE

Good-night. [*He goes into his room.*]

MATHILDE

Good-night. [*The woman listens a little. Silence.
Rises, goes slowly on her tiptoes to window, rattles the
window, and goes quickly down L. and sits centre of
sofa.*]

GEORGE

[*Enters. Stands just inside door*]: Did you call?

MATHILDE

Ah! . . . But this time you really frightened
me. What do you want?

GEORGE

[*With controlled voice*]: I thought . . . the
window rattled . . . What was it?

MATHILDE

Nothing. Only it's very hot. And so I opened it. [*Pause. Nervously*]: What are you waiting for?

GEORGE

[*Embarrassed*]: Er . . . er . . . perhaps this book—[*Takes book from shelf, facing door*]: . . . if you want to read . . . [*Takes a step to her.*]

MATHILDE

Go to bed at once! You bad boy! [GEORGE *exits into his room. The woman listens.*]

GEORGE

[*Enters again, coming to centre behind table*]: Perhaps . . . a . . . glass . . . of water . . .

MATHILDE

[*Breaks out laughing*]: I don't need anything . . . but come . . . kiss my hand. [GEORGE *rushes across to her and kisses her hand. Then he tries to kiss her mouth. She puts her right hand over his mouth. Pushes him aside tenderly*]: No, my friend, good-night!

GEORGE

Good-night! [*He goes into his room.*]

MATHILDE

[*Listens, rises. Crosses to table, blows out lamp. Crosses to* GEORGE's *door, R. Very low and scarcely audible*]: George! [*Silence*]: George . . .

GEORGE'S VOICE

[*From inside*]: Yes . . .

MATHILDE

Are you sleeping?

GEORGE

No . . . I can't.

MATHILDE

Are you reading?

GEORGE

No . . . I can't.

MATHILDE

[*In a low tone*]: Put the lamp out. Perhaps . . you'll go to sleep then . . . I want you to go to sleep! [*Lamp goes out in his room*]: Have you put it out?

GEORGE

Yes!

MATHILDE

And I'll . . . lock the door . . . now

. . .

[*She grasps the knob, turns it, opens the door wide and exits into George's room.*]

CURTAIN

END OF ACT ONE

ACT II

ACT II

[*SCENE: Same as in Act I, on the following evening after eight o'clock.*

The room is empty and dark. Outside on the veranda—just back of the window—a table is set for supper. On the table two large candles, shielded by glass covers, are burning. At the table are seated MOTHER, ROSALIE, GEORGE, *and* MATHILDE, *who sit directly opposite the window, the candle throwing a strong light on* MATHILDE's *face. Through the open window framed by the flowers standing on the window-sill, the entire picture has the effect of an old miniature painting artistically illuminated. Twilight. The room is dimly lighted by the light which shines in from the veranda.*

KATHERINE *is sitting on the sofa R., hugging two uncovered pillows. Her head has fallen on the pillows and she is asleep.* ANNIE *is lying sofa L., also asleep.*]

FRANCISKA

[*Enters from porch up R. Reaches the large sofa L.*]: A-o-h . . . my feet! . . . I'm so tired. . . . [*She tries to sit down.*]

ANNIE

[*In a low tone*]:   Don't sit on me!

FRANCISKA

[*Is about to cry out in surprise, but only a suppressed yawn results*]:   Ya-ah . . . Who's that?
. . . You? . . . What are you doing here,
Annie?

ANNIE

Just what you want to do.

FRANCISKA

What!

ANNIE

I'm lying down.

FRANCISKA

My feet . . . I can't stand up a minute longer
. . . I slept less than two hours.

ANNIE

Two hours! It was your fault that we missed the
early train! We all got awake in time. Only we
couldn't get you up till it was too late for the nine
o'clock.

FRANCISKA

We shouldn't have lain down at all.   For those three
hours .   .   .   And   that   sofa   at   Aunt   Marie's!
.   .   .   I'm still sore all over.

ANNIE

Serves you right.   It was your own fault.   Because
of you we didn't dare to lie down the whole day for fear
of missing the afternoon train too.

FRANCISKA

But we were home at five o'clock.   We could have
slept a long time, if we didn't have to wait up for Uncle
Gabriel!   [*She attempts to sit down on the sofa.*]

ANNIE

Go away from here!   Lie down on the other sofa!

FRANCISKA

[*Rises, crosses to centre, sees* KATHERINE. *Is
startled. Yawns*]: Oh! Annie! Katherine's asleep
over there!

ANNIE

Hasn't she got a right to be tired too?

FRANCISKA

Well, I suppose so! [*Crosses back to sofa*]: Annie! Annie!

ANNIE

[*Sits up*]: What's the matter?

FRANCISKA

[*Sits sofa again*]: Let's stick a piece of paper between her fingers and light it.
[MRS. FAY, *on the veranda, gives a loud laugh.*]

ANNIE

Go and lie down in your own room if you can't even stand a little dancing.

FRANCISKA

[*Seating herself on the edge of the sofa*]: Now listen . . . till six o'clock in the morning . . . and then that sofa at Aunt Marie's! [ANNIE *does not answer*. MATHILDE *outside laughs again*. FRANCISKA *looks toward the veranda*]: . . . Annie! . . . [ANNIE *does not reply*]: Annie!

ANNIE

[*Sleepily*]: What?

FRANCISKA

[*Looking steadily outside*]: Annie! . . . How do you like her? [*She inclines her head in the direction of the window.*]

ANNIE

[*Half asleep*]: Oh, lots!

FRANCISKA

And what do you like about her?

ANNIE

The mous . . . tache . . .

FRANCISKA

[*Taken aback*]: What?

ANNIE

The   two . . . points . . . are . . . so . . . sweet . . . [GEORGE *rises, enters from porch, looks round, then goes back again.*]

FRANCISKA

What are you talking about?

ANNIE

That good-looking Lieutenant . . .

FRANCISKA

And I'm talking about your Aunt Mathilde!

ANNIE

[*Laughing*]: Oh—Oh . . . Yes, I like . . . her . . . too—lots.

FRANCISKA

Well, I don't!

ANNIE

She is so handsome . . . and she laughs such a lot!

FRANCISKA

Well, what of it? Any one can laugh. But why does she put on such airs, here in the country? Since five o'clock she's had on two dresses.

ANNIE

Well, what do I care?

FRANCISKA

When we got home it was a white linen dress. Now it's a négligé.

ANNIE

Oh, you're just jealous! [*Turns over quickly, with her back to* FRANCISKA.]

Franciska

I? Jealous, because she changes her clothes? Such bad taste! Blue chiffon in the afternoon. Annie, do you think that would look nice on me? Annie, are you asleep? Horrid little beast! Pig! You look so comfortable. [*Rises, crosses to door L.*]: Well, I'm going to lie down! I don't care if I do muss up the bed! [*Exits L.*]

[*People on the veranda laugh.* George *rises, crosses to porch R.*]

George

I'll fetch it for you! [*Enters room, looks on table, goes back to porch. Calls*]: Mathilde, I can't find it!

Mathilde

[*Rises, protesting*]: No, no . . . I'll get it myself. [*Crosses to porch, enters room and drops down right table.* George *follows and stands right of her*]: Oh, this heat! Where could I have left my fan? On the table? [*Pointing to* Annie]: Oh, look here!

George

[*With suppressed, feverish voice, he tries to embrace her*]: Mathilde!

MATHILDE

[*Whispering*]: George! No! No! for Heaven's sake! Take care! [*Loud*]: Where can it be? . . . Oh, that's right, I didn't take it out of my trunk at all! [*She laughs*]: Oh, look, and there too! [*Pointing to* KATHERINE.]

GEORGE

[*Draws her to right behind sofa*]: Mathilde . . . just one kiss!

MATHILDE

[*Looks hastily at the window; she sees that the two women have their backs to her. In a low voice*]: You foolish boy . . . [*She stands close to him and kisses him.* GEORGE *embraces her. The woman slips out of his arms and crosses to left window; she speaks to those outside*]: Cousin Anna . . .

MOTHER

Yes, dear?

MATHILDE

Come here a minute, if you want to see something sweet!

MOTHER

[*Rising. Blows out candles*]: Come on, Rosalie, let's see what amuses them.

[*They enter through the door up R.*, ROSALIE *in the rear.* MOTHER *puts candles on shelf up right of door*]: Well?

MATHILDE

Just   look   . . .   Auntie   . . .   how   nice
. . . the poor, tired, little girls . . . [*Sits chair up L.*]

MOTHER

[*Drops down R.*]: Did you ever see anything like that! . . . [*Shaking* KATHERINE]: Katherine! Are you going to put on the pillow slips at once! George, light the lamp! [GEORGE *lights lamp above table, then goes up to right of window.*]
[KATHERINE *starts up, alarmed and half asleep, and drops her head into pillow again.*]

MOTHER

Katherine, are you dreaming! Get up and go to your work!
[KATHERINE *rises with pillows and exits down R.* MOTHER *crosses to centre.*]

ROSALIE

[*Has crossed to sofa L.*]: Yes, and here's Annie! What children! When I was a girl I could dance for three days without stopping.

ANNIE

[*Starting up*]: Who? . . . What's the matter?

ROSALIE

A shame to be so done up from a little dancing! Dear little Franciska's different. She can dance six nights through one after the other. . . .

MOTHER

[*Crosses to door L. Looks through the half open door*]: Hush! Franciska's asleep!

ROSALIE

Poor little Franciska!

MOTHER

[*Closes the door softly. To* ANNIE]: Go and help Katherine, my child . . .
[ANNIE *stumbles out sleepily through door down R.*]

ROSALIE

[*Watches her go, then sits upper end of sofa L.*]: You know perfectly well she won't help her! . . . She's going straight to bed. . . .

MOTHER

[*Sits lower end of sofa L.*]: That's why I'm sending her out . . .

MATHILDE

And that's why I'll send you out, and you too, Rosalie.

MOTHER

[*Laughing*]: Are you beginning again? I wouldn't think of lying down now.

MATHILDE

But there's really no sense in your staying up. Why, you can scarcely keep your eyes open. . . .

GEORGE

If you wish . . . Mother, dear, there's no reason why you shouldn't lie down . . . We will . . . [*Embarrassed*]: That is, I will . . . wait for Father.

MOTHER

[*Impatiently*]: Now leave me alone, do you hear! If I hadn't slept the whole week I wouldn't go to bed now. . . . [*Rises, goes up to door R.*]: I'm awfully worried for fear something may have happened to Gabriel. Why didn't he come on the five-o'clock train?

ROSALIE

He no doubt missed it.

MOTHER

Oh, I won't forget this Anna Ball for a long time. One surprise after another. [*Turns, looks at* MATHILDE—*smiles*]: I find you here, my dear . . . and your husband is in Gabroc the same time that we are . . . and we don't meet. . . . [*To* GEORGE]: What time is it?

GEORGE

[*Looks at watch*]: Ten minutes past eight.

MOTHER

[*Crossing up to porch, looks off R.*]: Father drove over to Gabroc three hours ago. . . . If he had met Gabriel, they would have been home long ago. If only nothing's happened.

ROSALIE

Well, you never can tell!

MATHILDE

[*A little impatiently*]: Please, Cousin Anna, don't be so anxious about my husband. I know him . . . he's not the sort of person that things happen to.

ROSALIE

No?

MATHILDE

It was quite unnecessary for Cousin Karl to have driven to town for him.   He'll get home all right.   And in the meantime we might all have slept.

MOTHER

But still I'm anxious   .   .   .   I have a feeling here inside.   [*The dogs bark off R.   Sound of* PETER'S *voice stopping his horses*]:   There they are.   Heavens, how glad I am they've come!   [*She runs out to the right, through the porch,* ROSALIE *following her.*]

MATHILDE

[*Rises, approaches* GEORGE *quickly*]:   George, my dear   .   .   .   now   .   .   .   now   .   .   .   my husband's coming.   .   .   .   Take care, dear, take care.

GEORGE

Don't be at all   .   .   .   at all uneasy, Mathilde. I know my duty.   [*Kisses her hand.*]

MATHILDE

[*Smiling   at   him*]:   Yes   .   .   .   Yes   .   .   . I know   .   .   .   I won't be disappointed in you. [*Voices outside.*]

GEORGE

[*Dreamily*]: Never, Mathilde!

[*Withdraws to the window.* MATHILDE *suddenly sits left of window.* MOTHER, *enters up R. with* GA-BRIEL, *arm around his shoulder.* ROSALIE *following.*]

MOTHER

My dear Gabriel! It's been so long since I've seen you! Well, you haven't changed very much! [*Turning him around toward her and looking him in the face*]: Only a few more wrinkles around the eyes. No matter. It's the same with me. We don't get younger, Gabriel, dear.

GABRIEL

[*Right of* MOTHER]: You don't age at all, Anna. Time doesn't leave any traces with you.

MOTHER

[*Turning to* MATHILDE]: Here's Mathilde!

GABRIEL

[*Going to his wife, attempts to kiss her lips. She turns away*]: Good evening, Tila.

MATHILDE

[*With great diffidence, at which she herself is surprised*]: Good evening, Gabriel. [*Rises.*]

GABRIEL

I've already heard of your fearful calamities. [*Comes down R. with* MATHILDE, *his left arm around her shoulders. Turns again to* MOTHER]: Anna, what do you think of us now?

[MATHILDE *breaks away and goes to R. behind sofa*]: When did we see each other last, Anna?

MOTHER

[*Up R.*]: Five years ago, actually, you bad man! [*She looks at* GABRIEL *critically*]: You've got a bald spot, too. Serves you right! For punishment. Because you never came to see us.
[ROSALIE *crosses, sits sofa L.*]

GABRIEL

[*Comes down R. C.*]: Ah, if I only had time! [*Laughing*]: But you . . . you haven't a single gray hair. . . .

MOTHER

[*Right of* GABRIEL]: I have whole strands of them. Only I know how to hide them. I already have a grown son! [*Crosses behind table to* GEORGE, *brings him down L.*]: Just look here! [*To* GEORGE]: Come on, what's the matter with you? Don't make me drag you.

[FATHER *enters from up R.*]

GABRIEL

[*Crossing to C.*]: Good Heavens! Is it possible? So this is Georgie . . . the little fat-cheeked boy . . . with the full-moon face . . . well, well, well! Do you remember how you let the balloon burst that I gave you? Do you still remember me, my boy?

GEORGE

[*Down L. His face looks gloomy, tormented*]: I . . . no . . . [*Quickly*]: I don't remember!

GABRIEL

[*Sits left of table C.*]: But a . . . a long time before I gave you the balloon . . . you rode horseback on my knee. [*Riding him again in panto-mime*]: Georgie Peorgie, ride a cock horse, ride a horse, etc. [MOTHER *laughs, sits left of sofa L.*]

MATHILDE

[*Impatiently*]: Oh, Gabriel . . . you're exaggerating . . . [*Drops down R., sits right of sofa R.*]: That isn't possible. . . .

GABRIEL

Yes, it is! Tila! [*Laughing*]: You don't like to hear what an old fellow your husband is!
[FATHER *is up R.*]

[GABRIEL, *turning to* GEORGE *again*]: Well, my boy . . . [*Rises*]: I'm glad to see you've grown up to be such a fine fellow. I hope we'll be better friends than ever! [*He extends his hand in a hearty manner.* GEORGE *hardly gives him his hand, returns the pressure not at all, draws it away quickly, and goes up to window, quickly. The others look at him in surprise.*]

ROSALIE

Well, I suppose he learnt that on the river!
[*The husband looks after* GEORGE *in surprise, laughs, turns to* MOTHER.]

GABRIEL

The boy is a little shy. [*Sits left of table.*]

MOTHER

Well, he grew up here. He's been all his life here on the Puszta . . . he hardly ever sees anybody . . .

FATHER

[*Embarrassed*]: He's not shy at all! Only obstinate! [*With a glance at* GEORGE]: And now, as I

see, he's pretending to be hurt! [*Drops down, sits chair behind table*]: I'll soon be tired of it!
[GEORGE *takes a step down and looks at* MATHILDE.]

GABRIEL

Oh, Tila!

MATHILDE

[*Suddenly to her husband it is clear that she wishes to change the subject*]: Why, Gabriel, where were you? Cousin Anna was very much worried.

GABRIEL

Tila, you don't know these provincial judges and lawyers, what a to-do they make out of such a case. It lasted until late in afternoon . . . But we reached the settlement that I and my Gabroc clients wanted. Then I had to go to the castle. [MATHILDE *turns away impatiently.* GABRIEL, *in a good humour*]: I have a little surprise for you, Tila. Well, you'll find out about it right away . . . I had missed the five o'clock train and my host was about to have the carriage harnessed for me . . . then Cousin Karl suddenly arrived . . . When I heard from him that you hadn't received the telegram . . .

FATHER

Just think of it, he runs off to the post office! And makes a row there! [*Turns to* MOTHER]: That's the reason we were so late!

GABRIEL

Yes, but I . . .

MATHILDE

You might have roared all night but the telegram wouldn't have been delivered until this morning.

GABRIEL

At the post office in Gabroc they calmly said to me that they had no night service. . . .

ROSALIE

Yes, but in town——

FATHER

That's right. There's no night service in Gabroc.

GABRIEL

But in Budapest they let me *pay* for the messenger.

FATHER

[*Laughing*]: And the messenger brought the telegram this morning.

GABRIEL

Don't you see, Cousin Karl, that it's a mistake to laugh at things like that? That's provincial! If they accept money for delivery from me, then they must have night service.

ROSALIE

Yes, of course.

GABRIEL

But I'll show the gentlemen! First thing to-morrow I'll go to the main post office.

MATHILDE

Oh, Gabriel!

GABRIEL

I will, Tila. I'll go to the Minister and to-morrow——

MOTHER

Gabriel, you don't intend to go back to Budapest to-morrow?

GABRIEL

Intend to . . . no, but I must. An important conference at four o'clock in the afternoon that can't be postponed.

MOTHER

But then . . . then you'll have to go on the ten o'clock train . . . [*Rises, goes L. to* GABRIEL, *pats him on the shoulder*]: Oh, no! no! I can't allow that!

GABRIEL

[*Sighing*]:   Unfortunately I must go, Anna.

MOTHER

[*In a joking tone*]:   Well then, go.   As it is, you behave as if we were only distant relatives.   [*Crosses to* MATHILDE, *embraces her*]:   But I'll tell you one thing, you're not going to take Mathilde with you. She's going to stay with us.   [*Sits left of* MATHILDE.]

MATHILDE

I'll gladly stay, Cousin Anna.

GABRIEL

You, Tila, here on the Puszta?   [*He laughs*]:   Yes, a day perhaps!   The second day you'll be bored to death, and the third day you'll hurry back to Budapest . . .   on foot, if there isn't a train.

MATHILDE

There you're very much mistaken.

MOTHER

Isn't he, my child?

MATHILDE

I should like . . . best of all . . . to stay here for the rest of my life.

[FATHER *and* GABRIEL *look at each other astonished.*]

MOTHER

[*Patting* MATHILDE'S *hand*]: Now that's what I like, Mathilde! That's our way! [*To* GABRIEL]: Not like you, you good-for-nothing metropolitan, you! [GABRIEL *turns, smiles at* ROSALIE. MATHILDE *looks quickly over to* GEORGE.]

MATHILDE

For the rest of my life!

GABRIEL

[*Laughing*]: You, Tila! I never heard anything like that from you before . . . you . . . on the Puszta. . . . They'll hear of this in Budapest. [*Humorously*]: What do you like so hugely here? [*Threateningly with his finger*]: Have you fallen in love with some one?

[ROSALIE *laughs.*]

MATHILDE

[*Quickly*]: Gabriel . . . what a silly joke! [MOTHER *laughs.*]

GABRIEL

[*Laughing*]: Or has the Puszta bewitched you?
Tell me, please. What has happened to you? I'm
really curious! . . . What has the Puszta done
for you? You were tired of Venice in three days.
[*He laughs*]: Well, well, well!

MATHILDE

[*Staring in front of her*]: I saw the mirage!

GABRIEL

[*With curiosity*]: Oh, really?

MOTHER

Yes! Actually. She and George!

MATHILDE

[*Quickly*]: Yes . . . when no one came from
Gabroc on the morning train either, poor George tried
everything to distract me. And so we went . . .
to see the mirage.

GABRIEL

Well . . . what was it like?

MATHILDE

It was wonderful . . . like nothing else in my
life. You can't imagine it at all, Gabriel. We were

walking in the sand.   The soles of our feet were burning   . . .   We had been walking for perhaps an
hour and a half   . . .   farther and farther into
the Puszta. . . .

GABRIEL

[*Incredulously*]: An hour and a half? . . .
You, Tila . . . on foot?

MATHILDE

Naturally we didn't take a taxi . . . [ROSALIE
laughs]: I leaned down to the ground . . .
George told me to . . . and laid my hand on the
sand . . . but drew it away at once . . . it
burned so . . .

FATHER

It's only when the sand glows you can see the mirage.

GABRIEL

Well, what did you see?

MATHILDE

First it was only yellow sand . . . and as far
as we went not a single flower, not even the smallest
blade of grass. Nothing. . . . And then sud-

denly . . . I was frightened . . . and dragged poor George back . . . for far in front of us, as far as the eye could reach . . . was the sea. . . .

GABRIEL

The sea?

MATHILDE

Yes, the sea. And in the midst were trees. Strange trees. And houses with fire-red roofs that trembled. And then the sapphire gleam of the sea rose in waves and came nearer and nearer, but when it was so near that I thought my feet would be sprayed by the water, then suddenly like a bubble it burst and there was nothing there only the yellow sand . . . nothing else . . .

FATHER

When a person sees the mirage for the first time it's truly wonderful!

ROSALIE

It may be for you folk in the country, but . . .

FATHER

Yes, but it's quite an event here on the Puszta. [*Rises, goes down to sofa L. and sits lower end.*]

GABRIEL

That must have been glorious, glorious, glorious!
And I am really glad that you saw it, Tila . . .
but that's no reason . . . [*Suddenly with a mysterious air*]: At least I think, Tila, you would be still
more pleased if it were the real sea.

MATHILDE

[*Looks at him, deliberately*]: The real sea?

GABRIEL

[*Still more mysteriously. Rises, crosses to R. C.*]:
Well, now comes the surprise that I just spoke of.
You must know that this Gabroc case . . . [*With
a jesting air of importance*]: that . . . hohoho!
. . . that was a big thing . . . a case in-
volving several hundred thousand . . . [*Explaining*]:—an expropriation suit between the Treasury
and the Gabroc estate. . . . [*Rubbing his
hands*]: It was a hard nut, but we cracked it . . .
the agreement we wanted was made . . . then I
went to the castle, to my clients and . . . well,
now comes the little surprise.

MATHILDE

Oh, Gabriel, you're making us very curious about it!

Gabriel

[*R. C. laughing*]: Just a minute, my dear, just a minute. [*To* Mother]: I must tell you what went before so you'll understand better . . .

Mother

Out with it!

Gabriel

[*Jestingly to his wife*]: I may, mayn't I, Tila? It's all in the family. . . . You see, Anna, there's been a little misunderstanding between Tila and me —[Mathilde *turns away impatiently*]—since the first part of the summer. . . .

Mother

Oh . . . oh . . . [*She threatens* Mathilde *with her finger.*]

Mathilde

[*In a bad humour*]: Does that have to be dug up now, Gabriel? [*Pouting*]: Well, if *you* don't mind it . . . [*To* Mother]: It's not my fault . . . Last year I spent the summer in Foldvar . . . the year before at Carlsbad . . . three years ago on the Lido . . . practically all suburbs. . . . Well, this year . . . [*Shrugging her shoulders*]: I said to Gabriel; either I'll go to Ostende or nowhere. Gabriel wanted a summer resort in the neighbourhood, so that he could come out each week end.

MOTHER

What! You don't spend the summer together?

MATHILDE

[*A little impatiently*]: But Gabriel has so much work to do . . .

GABRIEL

Pardon me, pardon me . . . if I didn't want her to go to Ostende, it wasn't on my account—I am not so selfish. [*Looks across to* ROSALIE, *goes upstage behind table*]: May I be honest?

ROSALIE

Of course.

GABRIEL

[*Laughing*]: It was because it cost too much money.

MATHILDE

[*Annoyed*]: Oh, Gabriel!

MOTHER

[*In astonishment*]: Yes . . . if there's not enough money why do you have to go somewhere for the summer?

MATHILDE

[*Shrugging her shoulders*]: You don't have to . . . as you see . . . to-day is the twenty-seventh of July and I didn't budge from Budapest until yesterday—all my friends have been away for weeks —at Trouville, at Biarritz, at Ostende . . . I stayed in Budapest. . . . If it suits Gabriel to have my friends pity me . . . [*Suddenly nervous*]: But why should we bore you with these things? [*With irritation to her husband*]: Why did you bring this up now, Gabriel?

GABRIEL

[*Slapping his pocket with an afflux of joy*]: Because Ostende is here!

FATHER

What?

GABRIEL

[*Pulls out his bill-fold and waves a large package of big banknotes*]: Here! There! Ten thousand! [*Puts banknotes on table for* MATHILDE.]

Mother

[*Taken aback*]: Heavens, you . . .

Gabriel

The Gabroc fee! [*Happily, to his wife*]: Well, this is the little surprise! [*Pause.*]

Mathilde

[*With sudden joy*]: Gabriel, are you joking? [*Rises, crosses to chair right of table and sits*]: You say before witnesses that I can go to Ostende . . .

Gabriel

If you want to.

Mathilde

If I want to! [*She laughs*]: I want it more than anything else in the world.

Gabriel

[*Happily*]: Well, so I'm selfish, am I? [*Sits chair behind table. Hands her the money*]: Here's your surprise!

Mother

[*Horrified*]: Oh, good Heavens . . . ten thousand crowns! And all that for a summer trip?

GABRIEL

[*Laughing*]: Perhaps not all of· it. But it will cost half of it.

MOTHER

Five thousand crowns! [*Still doubting, to* MATHILDE]: How many years are you going to stay in Ostende?

MATHILDE

[*Amused*]: How many years? Six weeks, Cousin Anna. That is, if the money lasts that long.

MOTHER

Five thousand crowns! . . . for six weeks . . . Oh . . . I . . .

MATHILDE

But Cousin Anna, Ostende isn't the Puszta.

ROSALIE

Of course·not.

MATHILDE

[*Calculating*]: This is the height of the season. Room and meals alone cost thirty crowns a day. With tips that makes at least seventeen hundred crowns in six weeks.

MOTHER

Oh . . .!

MATHILDE

And that's a low estimate. [*Quite absorbed in making plans*]: And then what's needed for the trip . . . I have nothing fit to wear.

GABRIEL

[*Laughing. Looking at* ROSALIE]: The poor child has nothing to wear!

ROSALIE

Poor darling!

MATHILDE

[*Feverishly, with shining eyes*]: And shoes . . . hats . . . gloves . . . a bathing suit . . . Oh, yes, Ill buy one of those smart little bathing suits when I get there so I'll have the latest thing.

GABRIEL

[*Gaily*]: And you're forgetting the most important thing . . .

MATHILDE

What's that?

GABRIEL

The desire of your heart . . . the Emerald Ring . . . at the jeweller's in the Waitzner-Strasse . . .

MATHILDE

[*Quite pale with joy*]: Gabriel! Are you serious? [*Takes his hand*]:
May I really . . .

GABRIEL

[*Shyly*]: That's why I gave you all the money! [*Puts his hand on hers.*]

MATHILDE

[*Happily*]: The Emerald Ring . . . [*Suddenly*]: But Heavens . . . if I'm going to Ostende . . . if I'm really to go . . . the dressmaker! . . . Gabriel, what day's to-day?

GABRIEL

Friday.

MATHILDE

Good Heavens . . . if I can't see her to-morrow, day after to-morrow is Sunday. . . . [*Impatiently*]: And July's almost over.

Gabriel

So, Tila, you'll come back with me to Budapest tomorrow? [*Laughing*]: Or are you going to stay here on the Puszta—[*Parodying her*]—for your whole life . . . to look at the mirage? [*Turns to* Father *and* Rosalie, *laughing. At the same time,* George *takes a step down, looks hard at* Mathilde]: She's going to stay on the Puszta her whole life to look at the mirage.

[Father *and* Rosalie *laugh with him, then suddenly stop laughing. Long pause.*]

Mathilde

[*Suddenly become serious, gazing in front of her, but does not dare look at* George. *Softly*]: Gabriel . . . take it back . . . it's safer with you!

Gabriel

[*Putting the money back in his bill-fold, surprised*]: Why, Tila, what's the matter with you? You've never given me money back before. What is it? Aren't you glad?

Mathilde

[*Uncertainly*]: Yes . . . I'm glad . . . of course I'm glad. . . . It's awfully nice of you and I do thank you.

GABRIEL

[*Out of sorts*]: Tila, no one can tell what you're going to do next. First you're glad . . . and now all at once . . . what is it this time? [*Sighing and turning to* FATHER *and* ROSALIE]: Good Lord, what's the matter with her? She has so many moods.

ROSALIE

Poor girl.

MOTHER

[*Rises. Crosses to behind* MATHILDE's *chair, and puts hand on shoulders, doubtfully*]: My, Gabriel! but now you're unjust!

MATHILDE

Never mind, Cousin Anna, I'm glad . . . I'm really glad . . . [*Gayly*]: I'm just longing for Ostende . . . [*Strokes her forehead, then suddenly in a tone which sounds sincere*]: But just now I'm tired. I can't talk about it now. I'm sleepy . . . and . . .

MOTHER

[*Taking* MATHILDE *over to sofa R.*]: Yes, dear, come over here and rest awhile.

GABRIEL

[*Rises, very seriously, follows* MATHILDE *over to sofa, pats her hand*]: Why, yes, of course . . . three hours wandering on the Puszta in the hot sand . . . and the mirage . . .

MATHILDE

We'll talk it over in the morning. . . . I'm so . . .

MOTHER

Yes, poor thing . . . [*Caressing her*]: You weak little city child, you!

ROSALIE

Poor darling!

MOTHER

But good Heavens . . . why, Gabriel, you haven't . . . oh, where's my head! . . . you haven't had anything for supper. [*Calling off R.*]: Katherine! Katherine!

GABRIEL

Ah, no, no, I daren't eat anything so late in the evening. Doctor's orders.

MOTHER

[*Horrified*]: Man, then you really are ill. You ought to take buttermilk five times a day! Lots of it!

GABRIEL

My stomach's a little out of order. I'm bilious, bilious, so much work, so much worry, I'm on a strict diet.

MOTHER

[*R. C.*]: But you must have something for supper. A couple of eggs, an omelette, a piece of chicken. You ought to stay here with us a couple of weeks. My good old-fashioned cooking would cure you. [*Turning to* MATHILDE]: You're not jealous, are you, Mathilde? We are old friends.

GABRIEL

Jealous? She? [*He laughs a little bitterly*]: Of me? [*Sighing*]: Rather I of her!

ROSALIE

[*Who has not sat quietly lower end of sofa L. "puts in her oar"*]: Well, you have a right to be! She's such a beautiful woman! That's the way it should be.

FATHER

[*Grumbling softly*]: Of course no one worries about me any longer.

ROSALIE

Well, she sees you every day. What do you expect?

Mother

[*Rises, crosses behind table to* Father, *who is seated upper end of sofa L.*]:   Good Heavens! . . .   You still have your new suit on.   Haven't even washed . . .   and you haven't eaten anything at all.   Go on in there.   The water's all ready for you . . .

Father

[*Rises, crosses front of table to R. and exits*]:   I can make good use of it, too.

Mother

[*Crosses with* Father *to R. C.   Stops and turns to* Gabriel]:   And you're going to be in bed in ten minutes . . .   [*She considers*]:   Wait a minute, how shall we arrange it?

Rosalie

Well, of course we'll give up our room . . . [*Rises, drops down left of door*]:   I'll wake up dear little Franciska right away.

Mother

[*Drops down R. C.*]:   No, no, we can't hear to that!   Just let poor Franciska sleep.

GABRIEL

Don't go to any trouble on our account. [*To his wife*]: Tila, where did you sleep *last* night?

MATHILDE

[*Pointing quickly at the large sofa*]: There, and I'll sleep there to-night, Cousin Anna. I there—and Gabriel, you here. [*Indicating where she's sitting.*]

MOTHER

No, I wouldn't hear of such a thing. Annie can sleep on the couch in our room and Gabriel can have Annie's room.

[*Goes to* MATHILDE, *putting her arm around her waist.* MATHILDE *rises*]: Well, we'll need some bed-clothes. Come on, child. I'll show you my linen closet . . . you can talk about that even in Ostende . . . [ROSALIE *exits down L.* MATHILDE, *hesitating a little, looks at her husband, as she walks up R.*]

MATHILDE

Yes, but

GABRIEL

Go on, Tila, you never saw so much linen together before. I remember it. Mountains of it. Mountains. [MATHILDE *and* MOTHER *exit through door down R.*]

[*Takes affidavit from his inside pocket, places it on the table and reads to himself.*]

GEORGE

[*As soon as he is alone in the room with the husband, he suddenly comes forward from the window to L. C., turns and looks at* GABRIEL, *straightens up and says with a firm, decided voice*]: Well!!!!

GABRIEL

[*Without looking up*]: Well . . . yes . . .

GEORGE

It's good that we are left alone.

GABRIEL

Yes, Georgie.

GEORGE

I have been waiting for this moment since you arrived.

GABRIEL

Mm—mmm. What is it my boy, eh?

GEORGE

I have something serious to say to you.

GABRIEL

Oh—mm—mm?

GEORGE

I only held back on account of Father and Mother.

GABRIEL

[*A little surprised at his harsh voice, but very kindly*]: Well? What is it, my boy? What is it, Georgie?

GEORGE

Well, first of all . . . [*Roughly*]: Don't speak to me that way!

GABRIEL

[*Pauses, looks up for the first time*]: What do you mean by speaking in that tone?

GEORGE

[*In a tone of enmity*]: I'm afraid we'll soon speak to each other in quite a different tone. But that depends entirely upon you. If you submit without protest, it won't be serious for you.

GABRIEL

[*Still more curious than shocked*]: Why? But what is it . . . what are you driving at?

GEORGE

You will get a divorce from Mathilde!

GABRIEL

[*His mouth remains open from astonishment, stutter-ing*]: What? . . . I? . . . from Tila?

GEORGE

[*Passionately*]: Don't say Tila! I despise that Budapest nickname.

GABRIEL

[*Can scarcely control his surprise*]: What . . . what . . . but . . . [*Enraged*]: How do you dare . . . that . . . I'll call my wife what I please.

GEORGE

My fiancée is not your wife!

GABRIEL

Of course not! What's your fiancée to me?

GEORGE

Your wife is my fiancée!

GABRIEL

[*Staring at him*]: Your fiancée is not my wife . . . and my wife . . . and my wife is your fiancée? My young friend, you seem to be a little touched. [*Touching his forehead*]: Ah, my boy— the heat—the heat——

GEORGE

[*Breaking out*]: Take care what you say, do you understand! [*With clenched fists*]: I'm making every effort to be patient, but if you abuse it . . . my patience will be at an end. . . .

GABRIEL

[*Rises, drops down to right of* GEORGE, *facing him*]: Mine is already at an end! What idiotic blither are you giving me?

GEORGE

[*Between his teeth*]: I'll tell you for the last time, take care! Another insulting word and I'll knock you down!

GABRIEL

[*Steps back in dismay*]: You knock me down, you knock me down! What! What! What do you want? What do you want?

GEORGE

[*In a hard tone*]: Mathilde!

GABRIEL

[*Cannot believe his ears*]: What?

GEORGE

[*With contempt*]: Mathilde is my fiancée and will get a divorce from you! Then I will marry her.

GABRIEL

Tila! My wife?

GEORGE

Mathilde, my fiancée! Do you understand at last? Mathilde loves me and despises you. So you will get a divorce and Mathilde will be mine. You must submit. [*Contemptuously*]: But if you don't want to submit, that suits me too . . . swords or pistols . . . or whatever you want.

GABRIEL

[*Stares at him a moment helplessly, without being able to speak a word, then he begins to shout at the top of his lungs*]: Tila! Tila!! Mathilde!!! [ROSALIE *appears at once in the doorway down R. Remains standing there.*]

MATHILDE

[*Comes running from the door on the right, agitated*]: What's the matter, Gabriel? . . . Has anything happened?

GABRIEL

[*Shouting*]:   Come here!   Come here at once!

MATHILDE

[*Crosses to right of table*]:   Gabriel!   Don't shout so.   We're not at home.

GABRIEL

I will shout!   I'll shout as much as I want!   [*Raging*]:   And if you tell me again not to shout I'll shout as loud as I want to shout!

MATHILDE

Heavens, Gabriel   .   .   .

GABRIEL

[*Left of table*]:   It's all the same to me who hears .   .   .   I will shout.   I have a right to.

MATHILDE

But good Heavens   .   .   .

GABRIEL

[*To* MATHILDE]:   Why, you, you   .   .   .

GEORGE

[*Trembling with excitement, down L.*]:   That's enough now.   .   .   .   Leave her alone.   Can't you see she's trembling?

GABRIEL

Trembling, trembling, you little . . .

GEORGE

[*Shouting*]:   Shut up!

GABRIEL

[*Raging*]:   You shut up! Who are you? How dare you speak to me like that?

MOTHER

[*Comes running in from door down R.*]:   What is it? . . . For Heaven's sake . . . what's going on here?

GABRIEL

[*Turning to his wife*]:   Tila, explain to me . . . how this fellow . . . [*Looks at* GEORGE *who grasps* GABRIEL'S *arm with both hands pulls him down to L., leaving* GEORGE *behind chair left of table.*]

GEORGE

I'm no "fellow."

GABRIEL

[*Struggles.* MOTHER *screams*]:   Keep your hands off, you . . . you . . .

MOTHER

[*Runs quickly to left of* GEORGE]: George, George, for God's sake.

[FATHER *rushes in from down R. in his shirt sleeves.*]

FATHER

What's the matter?

GABRIEL

[*Beside himself*]: Now listen all of you—— [*To his wife*]: But you answer me . . . answer at once. . . . How did this boy dare. . . . How did he dare to speak to me that way? . . .

GEORGE

[*Roughly to* GABRIEL]: Don't ask her—ask me!

FATHER

[*Down R.*]: George . . .

MOTHER

[*Left of table, wringing her hands*]: But for Heaven's sake, what is all this about?

GEORGE

[*Crosses to behind table, looks straight at his Father*]: I beg you to excuse me, Father, but *you* have nothing to say in this affair.

[FATHER *stares at him and is unable to speak for surprise.*]

GEORGE

[*To* MATHILDE, *tenderly*]: Mathilde, I can't help it! If this man dares to treat you like that. I wanted to avoid all this but now that it's happened, there is nothing else left.   Tell him to his face.

MATHILDE

[*Pale*]: But George . . .   for Heaven's sake . . . what . . . what are you talking about?

GABRIEL

[*Crosses to left of chair, left of table*]: Do you hear?   Tell me to my face . . .   he did!

MATHILDE

But what . . .   what?

FATHER

[*Down R.*]:   What did the boy say?

GABRIEL

That she . . .   that she's going to get a divorce from me . . .   that she despises me . . .   loves him . . .   is going to be his wife.   [*To* MATHILDE —*shouting*]:   That you . . .

GEORGE

[*Behind table. Very quietly*]: Well, speak, Mathilde!

MATHILDE

[*Breaking out*]: It's a lie!

GEORGE

[*Steps back, white as a corpse*]: Math-il-de!?...

MATHILDE

[*Raging*]: A lie! Everything he said is a lie!
. . . My God! Is this an insane asylum! Gabriel,
and you . . . you believed it? . . . Oh . . .
[*Collapses in chair, right of table, sobbing.*]

GABRIEL

[*Brutally*]: Don't cry! That doesn't impress me
any longer . . . [*Raging*]: Answer me now!
. . . How did he dare to do this? . . . If he
wasn't authorized . . . how did this fellow . . .
[*He involuntarily retreats a step.* GEORGE *stands with
bowed head and does not move.*]

MATHILDE

How do I know? . . . He's mad . . . [*Beside herself*]: Oh! My God! I can't stand it! Oh!
My heart. I'm dying . . . [*Sinks into chair.*]

GABRIEL

Never mind dying. I'm too used to that! [*Steps to left of table, raging*]: You . . . you . . .

MATHILDE

[*Rises. Crying hysterically*]: I won't stay here another moment to be insulted. I told you it was a lie . . . a lie . . .

ROSALIE

[*Crosses quickly to right of* MATHILDE, *turns to* GABRIEL, *faces him*]: But that's enough now, do you hear? Not another word now! She told you it was all a lie! [*The husband stands in silent dismay*]: I'm really peace-loving. Too much is too much! Just look what you've done to this poor little creature! Soon the little bird's heart will burst, it's beating so! [*Angrily*]: If she dies you're responsible. [*She turns to the woman, putting her arm around her waist*]: Come, my frightened little swallow. [*Leading her to door L.*]: He's a brute, like all men! For them we women are only here to be tortured. Come, my dove! [*She turns quickly, shouts over her left shoulder*]: Murderer! We'll leave them here . . . I'll take you in with us . . . Come on, I'll put you to bed. [*She leads her into the room L. and bangs the door.* GABRIEL *sinks into chair left of table.* GEORGE *goes up to window, his back to them all.*]

MOTHER

[*Crosses to L. C.   Softly*]: Really . . . Gabriel . . . that wasn't right . . . I must say
that . . .

GABRIEL

You don't know, Anna . . .

MOTHER

[*Shaking her head*]: Whatever it was . . . but
that way . . . you oughtn't to have done that.

GABRIEL

Oh, she's always fainting! That's nothing but act-
ing! But now I'm through! So that's what I won the
Gabroc case for! So that's why she wasn't glad!
She doesn't want to go to Ostende any more! She'll
stay here on the Puszta! I've stood a lot . . .
I've always kept quiet . . . but this is the end
. . . [*Quietly*]: To hell with her!

MOTHER

[*Moves up to his left*]: Calm yourself, Gabriel!

GABRIEL

[*Becoming more and more worked up*]: She despises me? All right! She'll get a divorce? **For all**

I care . . . [*He turns suddenly to* GEORGE]:
But she won't marry this young gentleman! I'll make
that clear to her!

MOTHER

Please be quiet! Mathilde already said . . .
[*With a sad glance at* GEORGE]: that not a word of
all that was true . . . perhaps the poor child has
lost his mind. . . .

GABRIEL

Hoho! They can't make me lose my mind! No!
I'll get the divorce and I'll show this gentleman what
honour is! [*Turns, looks at* MOTHER. *Pause. Rises,
crosses up to door, R.*]

FATHER

[*Up R. Blocking his way*]: Where are you going?

GABRIEL

To Gabroc . . . [*Turns, looks at* GEORGE]:
I'll find two officers who will act as seconds!

MOTHER

[*Crosses up to left of table*]: Good God, no!

GABRIEL

[*Turns to* MOTHER]: He must give me satisfac-
tion!

Mother

My son! . . .

Gabriel

Your son! [*Turns to* Father, *who is blocking his way*]: Get out of the way. I'm going to Gabroc!

Father

[*Has gained control of himself, with light humour*]: Not with my horses!

Gabriel

[*Taken aback, uncertainly*]: Then . . . I'll walk. . . . I'll get there! . . .

Father

[*Quietly*]: Yes, perhaps . . . to-morrow morning . . . if you know the way.

Gabriel

[*Stands there taken aback. At last gives up his belligerent attitude. In a boasting manner, turns, walks down R.*]: Very well, I'll stay. [*Sits chair right of table.*]

George

[*In a hollow tone*]: I'm going . . . away . . . [*He starts toward the door.*]

FATHER

[*Blocking his way*]: No, you won't!

GEORGE

[*Left of* FATHER. *Gasping*]: Father, let me go
away now! . . . It's better if I'm alone . . .
Let me alone . . . for if I stay here now . . .
[*Turns suddenly, looks at the husband, with clenched
fists*]—something's going to happen.
[GABRIEL *shows fright.*]

FATHER

[*Harshly*]: I'll be here, too!
[GEORGE *takes a step to him.*]

FATHER

You stay here, I say!
[GEORGE *steps back.*]

GEORGE

[*Breaking out*]: Get out of the way! [*Rushes up
to his father with his arm raised as if about to strike
him.*]

MOTHER

[*Runs quick to left of* GEORGE]: George . . .
your father! Oh, my boy, my boy.

[GEORGE *stands rigid.* MOTHER *draws him toward his room R.*]

Go into your room . . . we'll see about it to-morrow! . . .

GEORGE

[*Lets her lead him like a little child, at the door he sighs deeply*]: To-morrow . . . then . . . nothing will make any difference to me . . . [*He goes into his room.*]

MOTHER

[*Closes the door softly, pauses, keeps her hand on the key, whispering to her husband*]: Shall I lock the door?

FATHER

[*Up C. Quietly*]: The gun . . . has he got it in there with him?

MOTHER

The gun! . . . [*Her hand flies to her heart*]: Good Lord, he has it.

GABRIEL

[*Very frightened, rises quickly and runs across to L. and turns.*]

MOTHER

No, no, it's there by the window. [*Pause. Turns to her husband*]: Shall I lock the door?

GABRIEL

[*Quickly*]: Yes . . . tight . . . [MOTHER *turns the key in the lock. Very importantly*]: I'll show that boy——

CURTAIN

END OF ACT TWO

ACT III

Setting by Lee Simonson

Photograph by Francis Bruguiere

A SCENE IN ACT THREE OF THE THEATRE GUILD PRODUCTION

ACT III

[*SCENE: The same as previous acts. The follow-ing morning.*

ANNIE *discovered seated sofa L., book in hand, gaz-ing dreamily in front of her.* MOTHER *enters from up R. with small bowl of flowers. Sees* ANNIE *from porch.*]

MOTHER

Annie, what are you thinking of? You've been sit-ting mooning like that ever since eight o'clock.

ANNIE

Is it true young lieutenants can't afford to marry?

MOTHER

[*Who has crossed to table on veranda with bowl of flowers and has now returned to up R.*]: What, Annie?

ANNIE

[*Rises, embarrassed*]: Oh, nothing, Mother. It was just something in one of George's books.

MOTHER

Well, never mind about the book. Go and tell Father breakfast is ready. He's down there by the barn. Tell him we'll have it at the end of the garden, under the big tree. It's so pleasant this morning.

ANNIE

[*Crossing to porch on left of* MOTHER]: Sha'n't I say anything to George?—he's down by the summer house.

MOTHER

No, you get Father.
[ANNIE *exits through porch and off L. through veranda.*]
Katherine! Where's Katherine!
[*Goes down, exits R.*]
[ROSALIE *and* MATHILDE *enter down L.* ROSALIE *with right arm around* MATHILDE.]

ROSALIE

Anna insists on having breakfast out in the garden. Of course they do everything out of doors in the country! All those disgusting chickens picking around.

MATHILDE

[*Down L.*]: Rosalie, please close that door. [*Looking toward door down R.*]: I'm so afraid he'll wake up.

ROSALIE

I tell you he's down in the garden at breakfast already.

MATHILDE

Did he sleep?

ROSALIE

Did he sleep? He slept so well you could have fired a cannon right off in his ear. In his ear I tell you, and he wouldn't have wakened.

MATHILDE

Are you sure?

ROSALIE

I told you last night, didn't I, that men, those despicable villains, no matter how guilty they are, can sleep as peacefully as an unborn babe, unborn, I tell you.

MATHILDE

I didn't close my eyes the whole night.

ROSALIE

[*L. C. Laughing*]: You just think so, my love. Fifteen minutes after the great flood of tears you were asleep. You stretched so that poor little Franciska nearly fell out of bed. [MATHILDE *looks at her*]:

That's not why I'm telling you.　All you've got to do
is to look at yourself in the mirror.　You look so fresh
and rosy, no traces of a sleepless night.

MATHILDE

[*Down L.*]:　Yes, that is my unfortunate nature!
No matter how much I've been hurt I never show it.

MOTHER

[*Off R.*]:　Now hurry, Katherine, and help wait
on the table.

ROSALIE

[*Drops down about to speak.*]

MATHILDE

[*Suddenly*]:　But please go, hurry.　Tell George
to come here.　I must speak to him alone before the
others come.

ROSALIE

All right.　[*Crossing to R.*]

MOTHER

[*Enter down R.*]

ROSALIE

[*Up R.*]:　Good morning, Anna dear.

MOTHER

[*Coming from right, curtly*]: Good morning. We are having breakfast in the garden. And . . .

ROSALIE

[*Turning to* MOTHER]: I know, I know, and the dew isn't even dry yet! And those chickens . . . [*Exits up R.*]

MATHILDE

[*Crosses behind table to up R. C. Anxiously to* MOTHER]: Good morning, Cousin Anna.

MOTHER

[*Going up to porch R.*]: Good morning. . . . [*She doesn't look at her.*]

MATHILDE

[*Crosses over to left of her, stops her. Weakly*]: Please . . . don't be . . . so very angry with me . . .

MOTHER

I? I'm not angry . . . [*Shrugging her shoulders*]: Why?

MATHILDE

I don't know. . . . I just thought so . . . [*Suddenly*]: Please . . . I'm talking frankly.

. . . I want you to know it too . . . Rosalie
has gone to send George to me. I asked her to . . .
because . . . [*Desperately*] : I simply must speak
to him at once!

MOTHER

You? What do you want with my son? I'm not
asking what it's about . . . I don't want to know
what happened between you . . . But I feel . . .
that you have taken my son away from me. And, if
that's so, then God will punish you.

MATHILDE

But I want to give him back. . . . I mean
. . . I didn't take him away at all, really, if you
knew how innocent I am in the whole affair.

MOTHER

The poor boy didn't sleep the whole night. . . .
He walked up and down his room all the time and
ever since he got up he's been prowling about in the
garden.

MATHILDE

I must speak with George before the others get here,
and then . . . perhaps everything will be . . .
will be all right.

MOTHER

[*Pauses*]: Very well, speak with him and then perhaps everything will be . . . all right. [*Exits through porch and off L.*]

ROSALIE

[*Enters from up R., calls round the corner of the porch to* MATHILDE]: Hsst!

[MATHILDE *turns from the window*]: George is coming, my dear! Gabriel is still down there picking at his breakfast!

MATHILDE

Please keep him for a while. Talk to him. Don't let him come here while George is here.

ROSALIE

[*Walks deliberately into the room*]: Don't you worry, my dear. When I commence to talk to anybody, I've got a great deal to say. A great deal. Nobody can escape me. *Nobody.*

MATHILDE

Yes, that's very obvious! dear, but please hurry!

[ROSALIE *exits L. through veranda.* MATHILDE *crosses to sofa L. and sits.* GEORGE *enters from up R. Stands up R. just inside the room staring in front*

of him as if glued to the spot. Pause. Very quietly]:
George! Tell me, how could you possibly have done
this! How could anything so terrible occur to you?

George

[*Crossing to L. C. Deeply embittered*]　　I told
him! I spoke as I felt . . . sincerely . . .
with my whole heart. For I told you that I loved
you . . . adored you . . . that I'd marry
you . . . I'd die for you. . . . Of course I told
him. You ought to have known it, and you promised
that you'd get a divorce. You swore it! . . .

Mathilde

Listen . . . George . . . in such a case one
promises . . . and swears lots of things . . .
but . . . I never could have thought . . . that
you were so wonderfully naïve, and didn't know—
astounding as it is—that those promises can't be taken
with such dreadful seriousness . . . they can't be
taken seriously at all.

George

[*Left of chair left of table*]: No? . . . Then
what is to be taken seriously in life, if not even the most
wonderful . . . the holiest . . . the truest?
. . .

MATHILDE

That's all very beautiful and right . . . what you say . . . but think . . . what would happen if all these vows were really kept . . . all the foolish promises . . .

GEORGE

No, no . . . you oughtn't to promise . . . when you know . . . you won't keep the promise. There shouldn't be any lie about love. Not about that! Never! [*Sits left of table*]: You shouldn't promise when you know you won't keep the promise.

MATHILDE

[*Rises, goes left of him*]: George, perhaps for a moment I did mean it when I promised . . . Perhaps in the depths of my heart—but . . . no! no! George, it wouldn't be right—it would be too shameful to spoil your young promising life!

GEORGE

My life! I wanted to die last night for you, so that you'd see, so that you'd believe. I wanted to die . . .

MATHILDE

George!

George

Don't be afraid. It's too late! I didn't do it then; my gun wasn't there . . . they locked the door on me, and now nothing makes any difference.

[*Pause.* Mathilde *embraces him, putting her arms around his neck. Kisses his hair then rests her cheek on his head.*]

Mathilde

George, it breaks my heart . . . when I think of it . . . that you will love another woman more than me . . . Another woman will press your head to her breast . . . and you . . . you will kiss her. George! George! Never forget that it was my mouth your lips touched for the first time.

George

I'll never love again . . . never . . . no one! [*Crying out in pain*]: You've denied me! . . . And I believed you.

Mathilde

And I believed you, too . . . then . . . night before last . . . the happiest night of my life. . . . Ah, how beautiful it was! . . . and yesterday . . . on the Puszta . . . As I walked along with you, speechless, hand in hand, and

the sand beneath my feet glowed . . . and the air
burned . . . and the mirage appeared to us!
. . . [*Pause, suddenly in another tone*]: You
see, George! We walked on the shore of the sea of the
mirage . . . happy . . . carefree . . . then
. . . the mirage faded away . . . and now
. . . now you despise me for it . . . but I
love you. . . .

GEORGE

[*Rises, impatiently, drops C. front of table*]: Please,
please!

MATHILDE

Believe me, I love you! But George . . . you
see, you don't know life. [*Then with increasing impa-
tience*]: I must have the city, clothes and jewellery,
books and the theatre, conversation and lots of people
who like me. . . . Good Heavens, could you give
me all that here on the Puszta? [*Sits left of table.*]

GEORGE

[*Pauses, then turns, softly*]: No, I can only give
you my heart. . . . I have nothing else.

MATHILDE

[*Takes his left hand*]: Yes . . . that is the
most precious thing on earth . . . certainly,

George . . . But some day . . . later . . . you'll understand . . . Think of me then . . . that there are other things in this world besides love . . . and the Puszta . . . [*With great tenderness*]: The sea of the mirage is glorious, little George, but I need the real sea. The sea that doesn't fade away.

GEORGE

[*Takes a step down R. Slowly*]: Then go . . . go to the sea . . . no one here is . . . is holding you back.

MATHILDE

[*Rises, goes to his left*]: You . . . you're holding me back. [*Turning him round.*]

GEORGE

If you want to go . . . I won't stand in your way.

MATHILDE

But you are standing in my way.

GEORGE

What do you mean?

MATHILDE

I thought you were really chivalrous . . .

GEORGE

What?

MATHILDE

How could you do that, George, how could you do
that! Yes . . . I know . . . you dear,
honest boy. . . . You wanted to take me away
from my husband . . . all right . . . I understand all that very well . . . but that one
thing . . . that . . . that you shouldn't
have done . . . never, never . . . not that!
That never! Never! . . . Even if they had tortured you!

GEORGE

[*Pale with excitement*]: But what . . . what
are you speaking of . . . what do you mean?

MATHILDE

[*Pauses, turns away, goes down L.*]: Well . . .
even you must understand . . .

GEORGE

[*Crosses to front of table C.*]: What? . . .
You believe . . . that I betrayed my secret
. . . my only treasure! . . . [*With deep
pain*]: You believed . . . that . . . of me!
[*Shaking his head slowly*]: We don't know each
other . . . then . . . after all! . . .

MATHILDE

[*Doubting, crosses to* GEORGE]: No, George
. . . I didn't believe it . . . I couldn't believe
it . . . but my husband . . . shouted last
evening . . . that you had told him everything
. . . everything!

GEORGE

Everything . . . yes: that you despise him,
that you love me . . . that you would get a divorce from him . . . and would be my wife
. . . I told him that . . . But . . . my
secret . . . [*In ecstasy*]: If my heart was torn
out . . . if they . . . slowly tortured me to
death . . . if it cost me the salvation of my soul
. . . I would never betray a single word of my
secret . . . [*He straightens up, with almost childish pride*]: You don't know me, you don't know me at
all, Mathilde!

MATHILDE

George . . . if that's true . . .

GEORGE

[*Flying up*]: When I say so, it's true!

MATHILDE

[*Laughing, sits left of table*]: Well, then, George
. . . then everything will be all right . . .

then I'm not afraid any more . . . why, then,
Gabriel . . . oh it's much easier than I thought
. . . [*Suddenly*]: But you, George . . . you
must help me . . .

GEORGE

I . . . help you . . .?

MATHILDE

George, do you want me to pay for one evening with
my entire life?

GEORGE

[*In torment*]: What shall I do?

MATHILDE

[*Rises, goes left of* GEORGE]: Deny it . . .
deny everything . . . Deny even what you said
. . . think of some way. Say that you were de-
lirious when you spoke . . . that you were mad
. . . that you were crazy about me . . . you
didn't tell the truth . . . and I didn't know anything about it . . . [*Beseeching*]: But you
must say that *I* didn't know anything about it.

GEORGE

And you want me to lie to lower myself before him?
. . . Never! . . . I'll never do that . . .
Never!

MATHILDE

[*Goes down L.*]: Then my husband will cast me off. Your parents hate me, and if I had to stay here another day on the Puszta I'd die. [*Pause. Goes up to* GEORGE, *quite close to him, puts her hands on his shoulders and whispers*]: Tell me, George . . . Were you happy night before last?

GEORGE

Happy?

MATHILDE

[*Turns* GEORGE *slowly around to face her. Very quietly*]: For that evening, George, you are my debtor.
[*Voices of* MOTHER, FATHER, *and* GABRIEL *heard off L.* MATHILDE *exits quickly into room down L.*]

GEORGE

[*Stares as she leaves. Dreamily*]: I'll pay . . . for it . . .
[*Exits quickly into his room up R.* FATHER, GABRIEL, MOTHER, *and* ROSALIE *enter from up L. through veranda.*]

FATHER

[*Behind table*]: But Gabriel, you hardly ate a thing!

GABRIEL

[*Dropping down R.*]: I'm chilly down there in the garden.

MOTHER

[*Up R. C.*]: Not a thing . . . neither last night nor this morning . . . when can you eat, then?

[ROSALIE *stays up R.*]

GABRIEL

I'm not in the mood to have an appetite! [*Sits right of sofa R. Sighing*]: Oh, I had an awful night. You can't even imagine it. I didn't close my eyes the whole night.

[MOTHER *at window up C.* FATHER *left of her.*]

ROSALIE

[*Drops down R. to behind sofa R.*]: You're the only one who believes that, my dear. You slept very soundly . . . I peeped in several times. You're all like that, you good-for-nothing men. First you threaten to kill us, we helpless women, then you sleep peacefully. We women are different. Your poor, innocent wife didn't close her eyes the entire night.

GABRIEL

[*With a gloomy mien*]: Don't speak of her.

Rosalie

Don't speak of her! Well, I like that! What do you expect of the poor little woman? The poor thing cried all night like a rainstorm. Like a rainstorm, I tell you. It would have broken your heart, you bad man, if you had seen it. She kept crying continually: "Oh! Good God . . . I am innocent . . . I know of nothing . . . I love my husband. . . . . Oh, good God! Oh, good God! . . ." If you only could have heard it. . . .

Gabriel

Yes . . . if only that were easy to believe!

Rosalie

You can believe what I say . . . an untrue word never left my lips. Never.

Gabriel

Of course not . . . you misunderstand me, Rosalie. But if it's true, what you say——

Rosalie

If it's true. . . . Didn't I tell you she was crying the whole night long?

[MOTHER *sits chair behind table.* FATHER *drops down* L. C.]

FATHER

[*Slowly, thoughtfully*]: Well say, Gabriel, what do you actually believe about your wife?

GABRIEL

What do I believe? Yes, if I knew that exactly myself . . .

FATHER

[*Down L. C.*]: If you don't even know yourself, why all this rumpus?
[ROSALIE *goes up R., sits chair right of window.*]

GABRIEL

[*Nervously*]: That . . . that . . . you don't understand . . . this doubt is worse than the horrible certainty . . . but there must be something to it.

FATHER

[*Shrugging his shoulders*]: That will all be cleared up . . . in time.

GABRIEL

In time . . . yes . . . but I have no time. Time's just what I haven't got. [*Looking at his watch*]: Oh, what time have you? My watch has stopped. I didn't even wind up my watch last evening.   From that you can clearly see what condition I was in.

FATHER

[*Looking at his watch, goes down L.*]:   It's after half-past nine.

GABRIEL

And what time does the train leave?

FATHER

The Budapest express leaves at ten o'clock.

GABRIEL

[*Seriously alarmed*]: Good Lord! It's hardly more than a quarter of an hour till then   .   .   .   and I must leave   .   .   .   absolutely!

MOTHER

Ordinarily I wouldn't hear of such a sudden departure   .   .   .   but now   .   .   .   the way things are   .   .   .   I really don't know whether I should urge you   .   .   .

GABRIEL

It would be entirely useless. [*Pause. Looks across at the others.* FATHER *and* MOTHER *deliberately look at each other*]:   I must be in my office this afternoon at three o'clock. A conference that can't be put off.

[*Sighing*]: Yes, yes! My whole life is going to pieces here. My heart is breaking and I must go away! Because my clients expect me.

FATHER

[*Down L.*]: Well . . . if you can let your life go to pieces between two conferences . . . then thank God, you don't take the whole thing so tragically. [*Up to left of table*]: You see, it was a good thing after all to sleep over it.

GABRIEL

I really don't understand you. Who has time to-day for tragedy? Who has time for that to-day? I'll tell you something. Something interesting. I was thinking about it all night . . . or perhaps I only dreamed about it.

[*Pause.* FATHER *sits left of table.*] Yes, I can tell you . . . you heard everything yesterday, anyhow . . . and after all, we're cousins.

FATHER

[*Drily*]: Yes, we're cousins!

GABRIEL

Well . . . I suspected once before that my wife was deceiving me.

[ROSALIE *leans forward, looks at* MOTHER.]

People told me so many things. There was a good deal of whispering from good friends and acquaintances, too. . . . It was about a count . . .

ROSALIE

[*Quickly whispering to* MOTHER]: I told you so!

GABRIEL

Well, this fearful jealousy awoke in me, and since then it's never slumbered—never. For at that time a letter got into my hands and I was convinced that she was betraying me. What was I to do? What ought a man like me to have done? Well, I resolved to kill her——

[MOTHER *suppresses a scream.*]

ROSALIE

What?

GABRIEL

——And what broke my resolution? I ask you what? The letter came into my hands at ten minutes to ten in the morning . . . exactly ten minutes to ten . . . I had to start on an important trip at ten . . . It took five minutes for me to decide to kill her. *Five!* I happened to look at the clock. Five minutes to ten. I couldn't get to the court house with the tram in that time—ah! you don't know the Budapest trams. They're the . . . Well, I'll tell you about them another time. So I ran down and jumped into the first taxi that I saw. In the taxi I had a fine idea for the presentation of my case. I rushed into the court room a half minute before the case was postponed, explained my idea to the Judge, he hesitated—I won the case.

ROSALIE

Well, of course a clever lawyer like you . . .

GABRIEL

It was a doubtful case, a fee of six thousand crowns if I won it.

MOTHER

Oh, Gabriel!

GABRIEL

Now if I had gone on the tram I should have grumbled about the service all the way and would never have had the idea. So, I had to thank the taxi for that and I wouldn't have taken the taxi if I hadn't quarrelled with my wife. [*Pause.* ROSALIE *nods to him*]: As I got home and went up the steps, that suddenly occurred to me . . . [*Pause*]: and I didn't kill her. Ah, there you are! It's the little things that matter! [ROSALIE *nods again*]: One never knows, you see . . . as I was saying, she owes it to the taxi that she's still alive. Ah, you see, my friends, I haven't much time for tragedy.

[MOTHER *and* FATHER *look at each other and smile.*]

FATHER

Well, I believe that's your good fortune. In fact, the good fortune of most of us, that we have no time. [*Rises, goes L.*]

ROSALIE

[*Rises, drops down, sits right of table before speaking*]: And the letter—what happened about the letter?

GABRIEL

Oh, that was all a mistake. Tila . . . well, I mentioned her name and I never intended to. . . . Never! Well, Tila explained the matter later. . . . It was a stupid confusion of names.

FATHER

[*With deep humour*]: So there . . . and now think . . . if you had killed her!

GABRIEL

[*Slightly embarrassed*]: Ah . . . but that was quite a different matter. But this time, remember

please . . . a young man comes up to me . . .
and says . . . "Your wife despises you, she loves
me" . . . says he. . . . "She's going to divorce
you." . . . Now I ask you . . . explain it,
if you can. . . . Would the young man have dared
to do such a thing . . . if the woman hadn't given
him a cause for it? . . . No! I'm not as stupid
as that . . . I can't ignore that. [*Hesitating*]:
I must at least get a divorce.

[*Pause. Turns, looks at the others. They look
away, not wanting to object.* GABRIEL, *touched*]:
But then how shall I live without her? . . . For
I love her . . . I work only for her . . .
without her my life has no object. Isn't that so?

MOTHER

[*Softly*]: You . . . you must know that best
. . . Gabriel.
[*Pause.*]

GABRIEL

But that boy . . . you must admit that
. . . I can't ignore that . . . [*Suddenly*]:
No . . . No . . . I'll get a divorce . . .
I won't kill her . . . but I'll get a divorce.
[*Pause, turns again, looks at others. He waits for
someone to object. They turn away again.* GABRIEL,
seeing that it has no effect, takes out and glances ner-

vously at his watch]:   Good lord!   [*Rises*]:   Well, I
must go now.   [*Going up R. to door*]:   I've packed
everything.   I hadn't a moment to spare.
[ROSALIE *rises, crosses quickly to left.* MOTHER *rises.*
    GABRIEL *stops and turns.*]
    And she . . .   shall I leave her here? . . .
Or shall she come along with me . . .   or without
me? I daren't miss the train. . . .   [*Drops down
stage. Pause*]: Oh, very well, I'll go. [*Starts for
door.* GEORGE *enters from his room R. to left of sofa
R.*]

GEORGE

[*With rigid face, dull voice, quickly to the end, as
if he were repeating a lesson he had learned*]: I have
something to tell you all. . . .   Last evening
. . .   I did something very wrong . . .   very
wrong . . .   and now I must say so here.

FATHER

[*Up L. C.*]:   Well, what?

GEORGE

    Last evening . . .   I can hardly explain it
. . .   the heat . . .   the Puszta . . .   and
she was so near to me . . .   as we walked along together . . .   my head burned . . .   and the
mirage . . .   yes . . .   it was that . . .

now I know it was that . . . I thought the mirage was the real sea . . . and all that went to my head . . .

GABRIEL

[*Hesitating*]: Oh . . . if that were true . . .

FATHER

If my son says it, it's true!

GABRIEL

. . . But how did he dare? I don't understand that. . . .

GEORGE

I don't either . . . I can't explain it myself . . . something took hold of me . . . I couldn't help it . . . and . . . [*In torment*]: . . . and of all I said . . . nothing . . . is true! I didn't . . . tell the truth . . . last evening. [*Quickly in a hard tone*]: And she knew nothing about it! . . . Nothing at all. [GABRIEL *takes a step to* GEORGE.]

GABRIEL

Yes . . . but . . .

George

[*Breathes deeply, then almost shouting. Turning away from* Gabriel]: I swear that she knew nothing about it! [*He is silent and bows his head.*]

Gabriel

[*Beginning to rejoice*]: But then . . . then! . . . [*Quickly to* George]: Just tell me one thing more . . .

George

Please—please! I can't . . . Don't ask me . . . It's enough . . . more than enough . . . I can't stand it any longer . . . [*Drops down in front of sofa, back to audience.*]

Father

[*In a hard tone to* Gabriel]: I also think it's quite enough!

Gabriel

Yes, but . . .

Father

What more do you want from him? He's taken everything back. [*Sorrowfully*]: Oh, isn't it enough that he's humbled himself so?

GABRIEL

[*R. C., beaming*]: Oh, yes . . . it's enough . . . entirely . . . only that . . . [*His expression becomes gloomy*]: I still don't quite understand . . .

FATHER

[*Quietly*]: Youth, my friend! That's what we don't understand . . . as little as we understand the mirage.

GABRIEL

[*Coming C. step and looking from one to another*]: You . . . so you all believe.

ROSALIE

Didn't I tell you he was lying?
[FATHER *looks at them both.* GEORGE *exits quickly into his room.*]

FATHER

I believe, if you really want to take the train . . . you and your wife . . . then it's time. [*Glances at his watch. Goes upstage.*]

GABRIEL

[*Becoming joyful*]: So really . . . you think that . . .

ROSALIE

Yes.

GABRIEL

You can't all be blind.

ROSALIE

No . . . no.

GABRIEL

Then everything is all right! You believe . . .
[*He can't restrain himself any longer and calls*]: Tila!
Tila! [*Dropping down R.*]

ROSALIE

[*Going to door L. calling*]: Tila! Tila!
[MOTHER *and* FATHER *up L. at window.*]

MATHILDE

[*Enters at this moment with an excitement that she
evidently attempts to conceal*]: What is it? . . .
Am I dreaming . . . Gabriel! Gabriel! You're
calling me! Oh, Heavens!
[ROSALIE *supports her and leads her to C.*]

GABRIEL

[*Crosses to C., meets her, pause.* MATHILDE *looks
at* GABRIEL, *turns away, faces audience*]: Tila! I
don't know if I have a right to ask you, but can you
forgive me——

ROSALIE

[*Nods to* GABRIEL, *whispering*]: She will! She will! [*Then sits lower end of sofa L.*]

GABRIEL

——this time?

MATHILDE

[*Sobbing softly*]: Oh . . . you treated me so badly . . . when I think of it . . . I lay awake all night and cried. . . .

GABRIEL

Tila . . . believe me . . . I didn't sleep a moment either. I reproached myself terribly . . . that I had been brutal to you again . . . I know, I admit it . . . I tortured you . . . without a cause, as so often . . . but Tila, it all happened because I loved you too much. I promise you that I'll make up for it. Please forgive me. . . .

MATHILDE

[*With an occasional soft sob*]: Ah . . . If I just didn't . . . love you so very much . . .

GABRIEL

Tila, dear little Tila . . .

MATHILDE

[*Smiling through her tears, then with a deep glance, softly*]: Even if you had killed me . . . Gabriel . . . I would have died happy . . . in the consciousness . . . that you did it for love . . . [*She sinks on his breast.*]

GABRIEL

Ah, Tila! [*Happily to the others*]: You see, that's the way she is!
[ROSALIE *nods to him and smiles.*]

FATHER

[*Who cannot stand it any longer, roughly*]: But . . . if you really intend to leave . . . [*To* GABRIEL, *but by no means in an inviting tone*]: Or perhaps you have changed your mind?

GABRIEL

[*Breaking away from* MATHILDE]: No . . . Certainly not . . . We wouldn't miss the train for anything!

FATHER

Well, then, look sharp! You have scarcely more than five minutes! [*As he walks away*]: I'll have the horses harnessed. [*Up to porch, exits off R.*]

MOTHER

And I'll run . . . a little lunch . . .
[*She exits door down R.*]

MATHILDE

Just a minute, dear, just a minute! [*Goes L. and turns to* GABRIEL]: I must get my hat! Your Tila will be right back. [*Throws him a kiss and exits down L.*]

ROSALIE

[*Rises, going to door L.*]: And I'll go and help her!

GABRIEL

[*To* ROSALIE]: Oh, all right! Well good-bye——
[*Goes up R.*]

ROSALIE

[*Stops and turns*]: Not good-bye, only "au revoir."

GABRIEL

Not very soon I imagine . . .

ROSALIE

Oh, yes! [*Triumphantly*]: Our Tila has invited me to Budapest for Christmas.

GABRIEL

For Christmas?

ROSALIE

Yes, with dear little Franciska.   We're coming for two weeks.   Two!   [*Holding up two fingers.*]

GABRIEL

[*Sourly*]:   Indeed!   We'll be very glad!
[*Dogs bark, noises off R., etc.*]

ROSALIE

[*Looking in that direction*]:   There's the **carriage.**
I'll tell Katherine to bring the trunks.   [*Exits down L.*]

GABRIEL

Well then . . .   [*Calling to* TILA, *off L.*]:   Come along, Tila. . . .   [*Goes up R.*]

MATHILDE

[*Enters down L.   Crosses to C.   GABRIEL drops down R.   She looks toward the door of George's room, then at* GABRIEL]:   Gabriel!

GABRIEL

[*Suddenly realizing what she means*]:   So that you'll see what I'm really like . . .   I can't . . .   but you can say good-bye to him. . . .
[*Goes up to porch, exits R.*]

MATHILDE

[*Goes up to door of George's room, calls quietly*]: George! . . . [GEORGE *enters slowly. She goes to him R. then softly*]: Good-bye, George.

GEORGE

[*Softly*]: Good . . . bye . . .

MATHILDE

George . . . that was . . . very fine. . . . You are a hero. . . . I thank you. [*Pause. She comes closer to him, whispering*]: George . . . you'll come in the fall . . . to Budapest . . . And if you want to see me . . . little George . . . my dear . . .

GEORGE

[*Now stands face to face with her, looks her in the eye, drawn up to his full height, hard*]: The woman I love . . . can't be another's!

MATHILDE

[*Pause*]: Kiss me. [GEORGE *does not move. The woman, almost beseeching*]: George . . . [*She waits, runs her hand over his face to his mouth, for a final caress, laughs, and exits up R.*]

George

[*Does not look at her.*] Good-bye . . . [*Then goes up to window and looks off R.*]

Gabriel

[*Calling from off R.*] : Tila ! We're off !
[Katherine *enters from down L., dragging* Mathilde's *trunk. She crosses above table to porch and exits off R.*]
[*Dogs bark, noise of people driving away, shouting. Voices gradually die down.* Father *comes down from the porch to R. C.* George *drops down to left of chair behind table.*]

Father

George . . .

George

[*Quietly, brokenly*] : What . . . do . . . you . . . want . . . Father?

Father

[*In a quite different, more serious tone than he has used with him before*] : Look here, my son, I believe a little amusement would do you good.

George

Me?

Father

[*Softly*]: Perhaps, if you like to, you might go hunting a few days . . . or to the river. Go, if you feel like it. Even if you don't come home so punctually, Mother and I won't worry. . . . Or, if you want to go to Gabroc . . . to see some plays . . . You could stop at Aunt Marie's. I have nothing against it, either . . . if you take a trip for one or two weeks . . . say till the middle of August . . . a summer trip . . . or a few days in Budapest . . .

[George *looks down, moved.* Father *continues quickly*]: You're going there in the fall, anyhow . . . perhaps you might look around there a little first. . . . You are no longer a child . . . and I'm not worrying about examinations. [*Pause, then up to right of* George, *lays his hand on his shoulder*]: Now you ought to rest a little.

George

[*Ill at ease*]: Dear . . . Father . . . I thank you . . . for your kindness. . . . But I'm not going anywhere. . . . I must study now. But if you want to be good to me . . . leave me alone now . . . quite alone.

FATHER

[*Pauses, looks at* GEORGE]: As you will, my son. [*Goes to the porch, and exits R.*]

GEORGE

[*Listens tensely.   Sits chair behind table, staring in front of him*]: Now she's getting on! . . . My God! . . . [*His head sinks on table, his body is shaken with sobs.   He raises his head and gazes into the air.   He looks around, then his hand reaches involuntarily for his book, lying on the table, opens it and begins almost automatically*]: "The man . . . the man . . . the man . . ." [*He ponders for a moment, starts sobbing again, begins reading*]: "The   man . . . the   man . . . the   man . . . " [*Ponders again, then gives a jerk, supports himself on his elbows, presses his head between his fists and begins with a strong voice and grim accentuation*]: "The man who first gave expression to philosophic thought in the Hungarian language." [*Curtain starts to fall slowly, as* GEORGE *continues his speech*]: —"he who first dared to state that Magyarism, if it were to exist, must strive for a real national culture . . ."

THE CURTAIN FALLS SLOWLY